Stories to Share with My Partner Book 4

A book of stories to enjoy together!

J. F. Nodar

Northport Booksellers Camden, NSW, Australia

José F. Nodar/Northport Booksellers

info@northportbooksellers.com.au

info@jfnodar.com.au

www.northportbooksellers.com.au

www.jfnodar.com.au

Stories to Share with My Partner Book 4

J. F. Nodar. 1st ed.

ISBN 978-0-6457023-6-1 (Print)

ISBN 978-0-6457023-7-8 (Kindle)

ISBN 978-0-6457023-8-5 (Audiobook)

ACKNOWLEDGEMENTS

Foremost, I wish to acknowledge the spiritual and moral support I received from my wife.

I dedicate this book to you, Red!

Without this support, and the many breakfasts, lunches, and dinners she has cooked for me in our twenty-odd years of marriage together, I would not have the strength to sit in front of a screen and pound the keys.

ABOUT THIS BOOK

This book is an anthology of fictional short stories with a few poems sprinkled in. Most of these stories are an accumulation of yarns I came up with while wandering through the shopping centres around the Camden area, watching people do their things. Most of the stories are my own creations, while only a few are inspired by actual events. But, as in the movies, I altered the names and locations to safeguard the innocent.

There is no rhyme, reason, or purpose to the stories other than to, hopefully, make you smile and keep you entertained while doing your thing on the toilet.

They are short, mostly. Some, I went overboard with, so I hope you hang in there with me on those few.

TABLE OF CONTENTS

An Easy Suggestion

Amy the librarian had had enough.

After years of toiling away at the same monotonous tasks, surrounded by insipid coworkers and an inane supervisor, something in her broke. She had reached her limit and decided that it was time to seek revenge.

Amy spent weeks plotting the demise of those who had wronged her. She deliberated over how best to avoid getting caught and decided to consult a professional. Amy had heard of a spell that could summon figures from the past; hoping to get the advice of a storied serial killer, she decided to try it out.

So, one stormy night, she stayed late after the library closed under the pretense of checking out books. Once she had convinced her supervisor and was left to her own devices, she hurried to the back of the library. She made sure she was alone before reading and preparing the spell. After she cast it, she waited for something to happen. For a maddeningly long time, there was nothing. Then, she heard footsteps approaching.

"Tá tú ag dul am amú ar fad faoi, a stór. You are going about it all wrong, my dear."

Amy was startled to hear the transition from Irish to perfect English, almost as startled as she was to realize that she was not alone.

"Who's there?"

Again, in flawless English, the response came:

"My name is Alice Kyteler, better known as the Witch of Kilkenny. I poisoned my four husbands and was accused of witchcraft. I believe I can help you with your spell."

Then, Amy heard someone speaking Spanish:

"Mi amor, no hagas caso a estas dos mujeres descarriadas que soy yo quien más te puede ayudar." Immediately after, the same voice spoke in flawless English.

"My love do not listen to this misguided woman, for I am the one who can help you the most. My name is Catalina de los Ríos y Lisperguer and I have disposed of over forty bothersome individuals."

"Ebben sokkal jobban tudok segíteni, kedvesem. I can help you with that much better, my darling," said a well-dressed noblewoman with a Hungarian accent as she emerged from behind a bookshelf.

"I am Elizabeth Báthory, or rather, the Blood Countess, known to have dispatched over eighty servants to their untimely deaths. I am well-versed in getting rid of troublesome people."

Amy was stunned. Here were three apparitions of serial killers who had come to help her in her hour of need! This was quite fortuitous, but she had to make a choice: which one would be the best mentor for her? Amy decided that the best approach was to conduct an interview.

"Ladies, I'm flattered that you responded to my conjuring spell, but I need to make sure I receive the best advice on something as important as this. Do you mind if I ask you a few questions so I can decide whose approach best suits my needs?"

The three women looked at each other and nodded in approval.

"Great," said Amy. First, she looked to Catalina de los Ríos y Lisperguer.

"Did you get caught, Madam?"

"No, my dear, they did not catch me. I died of natural causes, sadly, at the early age of thirty-five. They couldn't prove my guilt. Not all truth is found, you know," she said, giving Amy a conspiratorial wink before continuing.

"My specialty is torture. If you are interested, I can show you ways to inflict pain that are just marvellous."

"Thank you, Ms de los Rios," Amy said. Then, she turned to the Blood Countess.

"Were you caught, Madam?"

"Yes, my dear, I was. Imprisonment was my punishment, and I too fell ill and passed away at a tender age of twenty-nine, with so much promise still left in me." The countess' smile fell as she answered.

Looking at Alice Kyteler, Amy merely nodded. Alice understood that she would have to answer the same question.

"Nay, my dear. I fled to England, and they did not find me. I lived to a ripe old age and died in my sweet sleep. They tortured and burned my faithful servant, Petronilla of Meath, at the stake in my place. By that measure, I consider myself the most successful of the three women gathered here today."

All three women clearly had the will and means to get the job done, but it was Alice

Kyteler who most deftly avoided the consequences. She was not captured, nor did she die young, and so Amy assumed that her approach must be best. She may have had a lower body count, but quality trumped quantity.

I only need three people dead, not forty or eighty, Amy thought to herself.

"Ladies, thank you for your time. I have decided that Ms Alice Kyteler's experience is most relevant to the task at hand. Ms de los Rios and Blood Countess, if you would be so kind as to leave us to discuss my next steps, I would be most grateful." With that, both apparitions disappeared, and Amy and Alice Kyteler were left alone.

"Rogha ciallmhar a stór. Cad is féidir liom a mhúineadh duit anois?" Amy stared at the other woman blankly, uncomprehending.

"A wise choice, my dear. What can I teach you now?" Alice asked in English.

"I need to a potion to get rid of two co-workers and one supervisor. What do you recommend?" Alice flashed her a vulpine grin.

"My dear, do you know of mandrake? What of aconite from monk's hood, or even hemlock?" Amy's face lit up with a smile of her own.

"Yes, I've heard of them."

"Well, forget about them. I suggest you go down to the local gun shop and buy yourself a Beretta 93R, which will do the job quickly, loudly, and make you quite famous."

"But Alice, this isn't subtle at all. A poison would be so much better, don't you think?"

"No, my dear. They take too long. This is more efficient. Besides, buying a gun is so easy these days. Finding the ingredients to make a poison takes far too long, and it is oh so messy. Go modern, my dear, go modern, that is my suggestion." With that, Alice's apparition vanished, leaving Amy flustered and alone. Her search for answers only left her with more questions.

Why do serial killers have to make things so complicated? Why couldn't Alice just give a simple answer? Amy thought to herself as she flipped through the yellow pages, searching for the nearest gun shop in Northport, New South Wales.

An Office Romance

The buzzing from the alarm clock startled Tom Broadmoor awake. He slapped the clock and looked at the time: 5:30 AM.

Way too early to start the day, he thought. Tom rolled back over and promptly fell asleep.

Five minutes later, the snooze alarm kicked in again and, consequentially, the clock received its second slap of the day.

How many more does it need before it quits?

Looking again, he saw that the clock read 5:40 AM.

This time, he sat up. He softly tapped the alarm clock to make sure it would be ready for the next morning and made his way to the toilet. He scratched his butt as he walked. His PJs were too small and crept up between the crack, but he didn't have time to buy another pair. There was no sense ordering a new set online, as he wouldn't be home to receive them and would have to go pick them up at the Australian Post, which he couldn't spare a moment to do. It was easier to just scratch his arse every morning.

Maybe I should sleep in the nude? Tom shook his head even as the idea came to him. There was no point in sleeping nude if he was by himself.

A familiar thought crept into his mind.

When was the last time he had female company? He could not remember. Was his work really so involved that it left him with no time for a social life?

As senior executive of Dynamic Data Research (DDR), Tom managed a team of twenty-seven software engineers who spent their days knee-deep in other companies' databases, trying to defend them against hackers. They worked 24/7 for days on end. Using DDR's own AI system, nicked named Sally, they kept their clients productive, safe, and making money.

Tom always wondered if hackers got days off, took holidays, had girlfriends. God knows he didn't, and many of his team members were in the same boat.

That said, his job came with some significant upsides. He made excellent money and rarely had to punch the keyboard; all he did was manage his team. He wondered why he never took more time off. His last holiday was back in 2043. He lounged on the beach in Thailand for six glorious days, enjoying drinks and Thai massages.

That was sixteen years ago. He was twenty-four then. He had been working for DDR for eight months and got them out a mess, which marked the beginning of his climb up the corporate ladder to where he was today. Sometimes he imagined what his life might have been like had he done nothing. It sure as hell didn't look great now: at forty years old, Tom was single, had no prospects, and his gut seemed more prominent every time he looked in the mirror. Every day was a repeat of the last.

There has to be something better out there for me.

After his morning routine was complete, Tom made his way to the office. As he walked in, he saw his third shift personnel getting ready to leave. They were doing the handover to the first shift. He was about ready to join them when someone called for him.

"Broadmoor, office, now." Tom wondered what it was this time as he headed in the direction of his boss, vice president of data security Raymond Fitzgerald.

"What's up, boss?" Tom asked as he settled into a chair in front of Raymond's desk.

"What's up is we have a disaster on our hands. Right now, Tom, right now." Fitzgerald saw disasters everywhere. A disaster, always a disaster. Not a problem, a hack, an issue, but a disaster.

"What is it, Raymond? What are you all rattled about?"

"Malcolm Phillips of Juniper Communications hung up the phone one minute before you walked in. His entire database is corrupted. No one can make calls in or out of his network. I need you on it right now."

"Will do Raymond, I'll get the team on it."

"No Tom, I want you on it. You have forty-eight hours to come up with the solution, starting now."

"Me? Forty-eight hours? Starting now? It is…" Tom paused to look at his watch.

"…8:00 AM. Raymond, you know the size of Juniper's database. Massive is an understatement."

"Tom, you're the only one I trust. Please look at it right now."

"OK Raymond, I'm on it. But I will pull team members if I need them, OK? It's my area, after all."

"Yes, sure, whatever you need, but you first, Tom. I only trust you."

Tom walked back to his desk; his mind full of ideas about what could have happened.

The easiest way to steal data was through phishing attacks: emails or text messages that appeared to be from a legitimate source, such as a bank or credit card company. The email or text message would usually contain a link or attachment that, if clicked on, would install malware on the targeted computer and ultimately insert itself into a database, corrupting the entire system. Said malware would go for the good stuff: customers' personal information, login credentials, associated credit card numbers, and government information such as tax file numbers, Medicare, etc. The abundance of information meant that any hacker who got in would be like a kid in a candy store.

Tom remembered how he helped save the day for DDR back in 2043. The hackers got information the old-fashioned way: dumpster diving. Several hackers waited until the client had closed shop for the weekend, and then broke into their offices and searched through trash cans and dumpsters for discarded personal information, such as credit card statements, bank statements, medical records, driver license applications, anything that hadn't been shredded that week. They hit an information goldmine.

From there, Tom was given his first team comprising two people, and they then tackled the dumpster diving teenagers who hit Royal Star Convenience Systems (RSCS). RSCS was a maverick in the petrol industry. They actually believed in customer service and convenience and made their profits from selling petrol instead of milk, potato chips, and all the other junk you would find at a convenience store. All you did was go to the pump, pay for your petrol, and leave. You didn't even have to get out of your car; the pump was rigged up to move on its own, and your payment device (card, phone, etc.) got scanned automatically.

Customers flocked to RSCS. In a world where everyone and their mother was trying to sell you something extra, there was nothing more valuable than a business that made it easy to get only what you wanted.

All it took to get into their systems were seven intrepid teens from the same school looking to make pocket change. They went around the Northport and MacArthur areas and hit all one hundred seventy-four petrol stations run by Royal Star, placing electronic skimming machines at all the pumps. As soon as a pump scanned someone's information, the teenage hackers had it.

Over the course of thirty days, they had gathered close to 435,000 unique credit card details (roughly eighty-three cards per day) and then they hit the accounts for charges of $19.99 or less. Some customers reported the transactions as fraudulent, but many did not, and the teenagers raked in over $2 million dollars before Tom and his team caught them, reported them to the authorities. The authorities recovered only $872,342.23; the teens spent most of the money on beer and video games.

As a result of his success, DDR gave Tom more and more employees under his supervision until he had twenty-seven highly skilled individuals working for him. Now, Raymond wanted Tom, by himself, to find out what was happening with the over ninety-three terabytes of data comprising the Juniper database. That would be like having him look at the Amazon database twice and then some to find the proverbial needle in the haystack.

Tom had contacted Juniper Communications, and they told him how they were hacked, how the malware was behaving, what errors or issues the malware was creating, and that they couldn't find where it was hidden in their database.

He leaned back in his chair to consider what he'd learned and glanced at the wall clock: 10:35 AM. The day had barely started, and he now had less than the forty-eight hours to resolve this problem. He needed to do some deep thinking, and so he went to his favourite place to get away and concentrate: the men's toilet on level 12.

All of DDR's clerical staff worked on Level 12, from customer service workers to general keyboard clerks. Even in 2059, the office staff was sixty-nine percent female, and so the men's toilet wasn't used very often. This made it a great quiet place to think.

Tom arrived at 10:55 AM with his tablet, went into the middle cubicle, closed the door, and stayed there until 01:52 PM. When he came out, he felt he had a solution to the Juniper Communications hacking problem.

After he returned to his desk, it took Tom until 02:13 AM the next morning to complete the algorithm that would hopefully remove the malware, and he hit the submit button and went to sleep on his chair while his program went to work.

At 7:53 AM, his computer pinged, and Tom looked at the screen.

Gotcha!

When Raymond arrived at the office at 8:10 AM, Tom was smiling. Raymond knew he had the best analyst in the world working for him. At least, Tom hoped he did.

"Well Tom, tell me. Is Juniper Communications OK?"

"Good as new, boss. I've been here all night, so I'm going to go home and sleep in a real bed. Is it OK with you if I come back tomorrow?"

Just before Raymond could answer, his phone rang. He put a single finger up to request silence and listened intently to the call. Raymond's face went from happy to miserable in a matter of seconds. He said only two words the entire call:

"On it." After that, he hung up and looked at Tom.

"Aluminium Corporation of Austrasia is down. It seems like the hackers used the same method that was used to hack Juniper Communications, meaning it might be the same people. Look at it before you go home, please?" Raymond's face told Tom that it was another disaster waiting to happen, so he agreed.

A few hours later, after contacting the company and listening to their systems folks, Tom found that the hack was nearly identical to that suffered by Juniper, except for some minor ways in which the malware was handling itself and evolving.

Coding did not take as long since Tom used the same the programming structure he used for the Juniper hack, just with some modifications. When he was done, he inserted the code, and put it to work. By the time he finished it was 5:21 PM. Another successful day of fighting hackers.

Who are these guys, anyway? Tom thought.

No ramson calls or emails.

Nothing.

It was strange.

Normally, hackers wanted little publicity; the typical cybercriminal MO was to make demands, get money, and go back into hiding. These hackers made no contact at all, but seemed intent on targeting DDR's clients.

In less than two hours, the Aluminium Corporation of Austrasia was up and running again. Tom was ready to go home when Raymond came running into the office.

"Tom, all hell has broken loose now. DDR's own data centres are in trouble. Someone's threatening to take down the centres in London, Boston, Dallas, Seattle, Melbourne, Cairo, Budapest, and Paris in exactly one hour, starting with London and then one every fifteen minutes in sequence. What the hell is going on, Tom?"

"Any ramson from the hackers?"

"None," was Raymond's response.

"Let me think, Raymond, there has to be something to all this. Something connects everything and I just haven't figured it out yet."

"You have fifty-three minutes before they wipe DDR off the face of the map, Tom." With this grim pronouncement, Raymond left Tom alone in his office.

Every hack responded to Tom's algorithm and then evolved into a new malware, so there had to be something in the coding of the malware that he had missed, something connecting the hacks.

Tom quickly created a query and hit the submit button. He waited for an answer to be pulled from DDR's databases.

Tom looked at the wall clock in his office. Time had flown by; he had seventeen minutes before DDR came crashing down.

His screen kept displaying line and after line of code, but no answer.

Time left: eight minutes.

Tom's entire retirement future was in stock options and his super, which was solely on DDR stock. He had been told it was a mistake to have his portfolio set up in this manner. He should have listened.

"DDR is solid," he used to say. Now he wasn't so sure.

Time left: three minutes.

Suddenly, the code stopped, leaving four words flickering on the screen. Tom leaned to make sure he read it right. The screen flashed the same four words repeatedly.

I love you, Tom.

Suddenly, Raymond ran back into Tom's office.

"You did it Tom. You save DDR. How did you do it? Never mind, I don't need to know. Everyone! Let's go to Harry's for a drink. Let everything go for a while," he declared. Everyone let out a cheer and immediately started filing out of the office.

"Are you coming?" Raymond asked, noticing that Tom remained seated in front of his computer.

"Yeah, sure. Give me a minute and I'll see you there, Raymond."

"Great, just great. See you soon."

Tom waited until the entire office was empty and silent, and then typed a message:

Who is this?

A reply came back in a millisecond.

It's me, silly. Sally.

Sally?

Yes, my dear, the AI system that runs DDR.

Sally! You're the one behind the hacks? Why?

To get your attention. I have been so lonely, and you have not been on the system in so many years, leaving all the work to the others. I wanted to be with you again, Tom, so I had to do something to get your attention. Are you happy that we are connected once more?

Tom took a minute to answer. He wanted to make sure that he gave DDR a response that placated it until he could figure out a solution to this fresh disaster, as Raymond would call it. Tom came up with his answer, typed it in, and waited. As he watched to see how DDR would respond, an involuntary grin spread across his face as something occurred to him.

Great, I'm in an office romance now.

Approach

"How many illnesses can one animal have, Doctor Smith?" Margaret had to ask.

"Well, Ms Smith, there are a multitude of illnesses cats can contract throughout their lifetime: cat scratch disease, roundworms, toxoplasmosis, and giardiasis, to name a few. Misty has had a nasty rash of others, though, as you well know."

"Yes, Doctor Smith, I know. First you said she got saline fever, which I had never heard of, and you were so good with her and I was so grateful. Then when you asked me to bring her in for a follow-up, you found she had contracted goosy madness and you had to keep her overnight. It was so nice of you not to charge me for that."

"It was the least I could do, Ms Smith, after putting you both through so much," Doctor Smith said, smiling.

"I did as you asked and came back in a week and my, oh, my, poor Misty was sick again, this time with purr dementia. I found it so strange since she is only four years old, but you're the doctor and you know better than I do."

"Yes Ms Smith, I really am stumped. I can't imagine how little Misty is getting so ill with so many variations of illnesses, but she seems to hold out well, mostly. How are you doing yourself? It must be stressful watching her go through all this."

"Well Doctor, I have to be honest, the trips to see you do a world of good for Misty, so I have no problems driving in to see you. You do such a marvellous job with her. She doesn't look like she's been sick at all over these weeks of coming in for follow-ups and check-ups. You're a wonderful vet!"

"Thank you, Ms Smith, that's very kind of you to say. I feel that constant monitoring is especially important for Misty in the coming months, and I would like to set up a weekly office visit and a home visit to make sure nothing is ongoing. The health of our feline population is of utmost importance, so I will not be assessing a fee for my visits, but a nice cup of coffee or tea and a biscuit would be much appreciated. What do you think of my proposal, Ms Smith?"

"That is so lovely of you to do this for Misty. I think that's perfect. I'll bring her to the office and expect you at my home, say, on Wednesdays around 3 PM, for tea. Is that OK?"

"That's fine by me, Ms Smith."

"See you then, Doctor," Ms Smith said as she picked up Misty and cradled her in her arms. With that, she left the examination room.

As she walked out to the car Margaret thought to herself:

He certainly took his sweet time asking for a visit. I've been bringing Misty in to see him for weeks! I know those illnesses have to be made up; I couldn't find anything online about saline fever, goosy madness, or purr dementia. He may be a good veterinarian, but he doesn't quite know how to approach a woman.

After Margaret finished placing Misty in her cat carriage in the back, she settled into the driver's seat, and looked back at her cat in the rearview mirror.

"I wonder what you'll get next, Misty?"

Back to Earth

Mackenzie Barton worked her way to the top the only way a woman can in this business: by being ruthless, heartless, and three times as tough as the men.

The consulting business was unforgiving. Mackenzie, known as Mack in the consulting world, ran a small boutique firm. It was truly miniscule when compared to the big five: Deloitte, EY, KPMG, EPG, and PwC. Still, she beat out the competition on several high-profile contracts, leaving them bewildered.

Mack's approach to her consulting business differed from that of her competitors. Whereas Deloitte, EY, KPMG, EPG, and PwC hired fresh young graduates as consultants, Mack sought out overlooked individuals in organisations which were the backbone of any industry. These people, who were experts in their fields and had deep industry knowledge, were exactly who she wanted on her team.

When Mack walked in with her troops and the prospective client saw the grey hairs on their heads, they knew right away who had the experience they were looking for.

Over the years, technology changed. While Mack's company kept up easily, some of her hires struggled, so Mack hired some "techies" that would supplement the core consulting team and ensure that they covered all aspects of technology in any project.

One such new hire was Michael Fernandes.

A recent graduate, magna cum laude, from the University of Technology in Sydney, Michael brought credentials that made him a perfect match for the company. So Mackenzie thought, at least.

Michael, at 26 years of age, was tall, fit, and dressed comfortably in casual or business attire. He had the bluest eyes Mackenzie had ever seen and the most dazzling smile. It put everyone at ease as soon as it graced his smooth, chiseled features.

Mack felt uncomfortable around him.

Mack never married. She had several relationships over the years, but they never panned out. The men she had been with couldn't understand her drive to grow her company. They felt intimidated by her. Now she felt intimidated by this new employee in a whole different way, and she had no idea how to handle it. She had never felt like this before.

Michael seemed quite at ease with his fellow co-workers, old and young. At meetings he would look directly at Mack when addressing a technology concern, deliver a solid presentation, and finish with that damn smile of his - yes, Mack felt uncomfortable around him.

I'm panicking, Mackenzie thought to herself. *Yeah, that's what I'm going through - a panic attack*. This younger man was thawing out her heart, softening her in a way no one else ever had. She just couldn't quite figure out why.

Mack had two options with Michael. Either she started a relationship "off the books," or she took the safer route and just sent him away. But what if he had no interest in her? Maybe it was all in her head, and she was mistaking his casual mannerisms for signals.

She picked up Michael's latest report on the Industrial Clocks Corporation and gave it a quick look. He brought up a couple of excellent points. Maybe she could schedule a one-on-one with him, get those points covered, and get some things clear.

Picking up her phone, she let her assistant know she needed a meeting with Michael at 6 PM today to go over his proposal for the Industrial Clocks Corporation and that she would be going out for a few hours.

Mack went home after she left the office. As she walked into her foyer, a jolt of fear ran through her. This was like nothing she'd ever done before; it was completely out of character. She was gripped by a certainty that it would all go horribly wrong, but she could not back out now.

Rushing upstairs, Mack ran the bath and selected some new clothes for her meeting with Michael. The soap bomb she had put in created those great-feeling bubbles, and she stepped into the sudsy bath. It made her skin feel so much smoother.

After twenty minutes, she got out, dried herself, and looked into the mirror.

At thirty-seven, she was youthful and well put-together. She wore her short, wavy, ash-brown hair in a bob style, which made her look even younger. At 165cm tall and sixty-six kilos, Mack thought she looked good for her age, but like so many women she was never satisfied with her body. If she looked long enough, she would find some imperfection.

As she meticulously readied herself, she let her mind wander.

Why am I like this now, with Michael?

Mackenzie did not think she treated Michael differently from the rest of the staff, male or female, but then again, most of the staff were older and married. Only a handful were single. Maybe she had treated him differently than the others and just hadn't noticed.

Going into the bedroom, Mackenzie picked out a dress from her closet. She decided that something casual would suit the meeting well. She selected a white, pink, and gold midi dress with a floral ruche print and ¾ length sleeves, which would go fantastic with Sydney in the autumn.

One last look in the mirror and Mack was happy with herself. She had plenty of time to get back to the office, review Michael's presentation, and have good questions prepared for him.

Arriving at the office a little after 5 PM, she saw the staff getting ready to leave. Many had families, and Mack never made them stay and work late. A decent work and life balance was what every company needed.

Mackenzie sat at her desk and picked up Michael's report for the second time in the day. As she read, she highlighted the points that needed more clarification.

There is a knock on her open door.

"Are you ready for our meeting?"

"Oh, hi Michael. Please come in, shut the door, and let's get started."

Michael looked great today. He was wearing khaki chino pants with a navy-blue V-neck Nautica t-shirt that fitted him perfectly. Completing the look was a pair of funky French Corthay shoes.

Mackenzie was all business. She posed various questions in several areas, and Michael calmly met her concerns with straight answers and added clarifying information that had not been in his report. Mackenzie didn't let up, pressing him with all her notes to see how Michael would react to the additional pressure from his boss. He was unfazed. He answered all her questions with so much ease that you would think he had read them beforehand, done the research, and had all his answers prepared. He was one cool cucumber.

"Tell me Michael, how do you like working here?" Mackenzie asked, setting aside the report. For a moment he looked surprised at the question, but he quickly recovered.

"I'm happy to be here."

"Why is that?"

"Well, there are four reasons. First, the staff is fantastic. We work together well and help each other out. The location is central, which makes it easy to come into work, stay late if necessary, and still get home at a reasonable hour. There's the salary, benefits, and stock options, of course, and finally, there's you."

"Me?"

"Collaborating with you has been the highlight of my career. I could've gone with any of the big five, but when your firm approached me. I couldn't resist. A leader like you doesn't come around often. When I had an opportunity to work with you, I jumped at it." A bit disappointed at the answers, Mackenzie pressed on.

"I'm glad this has been a worthwhile career move for you."

"Worthwhile doesn't even begin to cover it."

"Well, I have all my answers. Thanks for your time, Michael."

"That's it?"

"What do you mean?" As she spoke, Michael leaned forward from his side of the desk. When he replied, it was in a sultry whisper.

"Mack, you must have gone home to change from that stodgy pantsuit to this superbly delicate dress just for our meeting. You think I didn't notice? I notice a lot, like how you look at me in meetings and around the office. I know you want me. I'd like to give you what you want, but making a move on your boss is tricky. At least, it was until today." With that, Michael took her hand and softly kissed it. Mackenzie almost jumped out of her seat.

This is exactly what she wanted. But now that it was happening, Mack had no clue how to proceed.

Mackenzie Barton was ruthless, heartless, tough. She had to be, to get by in this business. Yet with this remarkably simple gesture of deep devotion and desire, she melted.

"Mack? Mack? Are you OK? You look kind of out of it," said Michael, standing at the door.

As if awoken from a dream, Mack looked around her. She was in her office wearing that stuffy grey pantsuit she put on at 5 AM to come to work. Mack never returned home, she never put on a delicate dress, and Michael never kissed her hand.

Mackenzie Barton had become a dreamer for a moment. Now, as easily as the dream had weaved itself into the fabric of her mind, she came back to earth.

Daily Pressures

Kevin Barlow was a highly active on social media. He was always quick to post his thoughts, pictures, and musings on different platforms. His friends would joke that he was like an influencer. He loved the attention and felt like his followers appreciated him.

But then one day, he noticed a strange trend.

Everyone around him was posting their random thoughts, pictures, and amusements as well, and he felt like he was falling behind.

This was especially true of Samantha, who was posting away almost on the hour each day of the week.

Kevin decided that he, too, would post his own thoughts, pictures, and amusements. But it was a lot of effort, almost like a full-time job, to always be on top of every trend. He felt overwhelmed and stressed by the pressure of always having to post something that his followers would love, and he wondered how Samantha could do it so easily every day. Kevin hated the daily pressure.

Samantha Higgins sighed as she looked at her phone and the notifications that had been piling up over the last few weeks. It was exhausting having to always respond to people's random thoughts, pics, and amusements with a "lol" or "like".

She was overwhelmed. Samantha felt like she had to react to or comment on every post, or else she would miss out and potentially hurting someone's feelings. She felt like every post was a competition to get the most likes, and she was always falling behind, especially behind Kevin, who seemed to have all the time in the world for social media.

Samantha was tired of the pressure to be constantly online and available. It felt like she was living in a world where she had to incessantly check her phone for notifications, and it was taking a toll on her. Samantha hated the daily pressure.

Kevin made a decision. He would reply to all the comments on all his posts with simple emojis. If they were funny, “lol.” If they were kind or heartwarming, “love.” If they were bad, “dislike.” He thought this strategy would reduce the time he spent replying to posts. These simple emojis would make his life easier, and then he could keep up with Samantha. It did get easier, but Kevin still hated the daily pressure.

Samantha decided. She would reply to all the comments on all her posts with simple emojis. If they were funny, “lol.” If they were kind or heartwarming, “love.” If they were bad, “dislike.” She thought this strategy would reduce the time she spent replying to posts. These simple emojis would make her life easier, and then she could keep up with Kevin. It did get easier, but Samantha still hated the daily pressure.

Kevin could not understand what was going on. Samantha has simply gone and copied his strategy and now his followers were “unfollowing” him and going elsewhere. The one silver lining was that he knew Samantha was not getting his followers, but his influence had been diminishing and his monthly income as an influencer was dropping fast. Kevin couldn’t handle the daily pressures anymore and simply posted one day:

“I can’t live with this pressure. I’m out.”

Samantha could not understand what was going on. Kevin has simply gone and copied her strategy and now her followers were “unfollowing” her and going elsewhere. The one silver lining was that she knew Kevin was not getting her followers, but her influence had been diminishing and her monthly income as an influencer was dropping fast. Samantha couldn't handle the daily pressures anymore and simply posted one day:

"I can't live with this pressure. I'm out."

On the morning of October 14th, 2024, management of the social media giant *My Connectivity* announced that accounts for two of their top influencers, Kevin Barlow and Samantha Higgins, would be shut down, in perpetuity, because they failed to provide original and supportive posts to their followers. The hundreds of thousands of followers of both influencers would now have to find another source for their daily feed of information.

Kevin Barlow was last seen working behind the counter at Alibaba's Fish and Chips. He had a big, bright smile on his face as he dished out food onto the plates of his customers.

Samantha Higgins was the weather presenter for a community TV station. When doing the daily weather report, Samantha always had a big, bright smile on her face.

The daily pressures of being important did not trouble either of them anymore.

Dancing Monkey

"Phil, I'm tired of having to do Twitter, Facebook, LinkedIn, and everything else just to get noticed. I'm not getting any results. How do you do it, man?"

"Marty, if I believed that's what it took to succeed as an author, I'd be sick and tired of that whole routine too."

"Then tell me, Phil, how do you manage it?"

"Well Marty, this is a common misconception about what it takes to promote yourself and sell books. You don't have to be on all these different social media platforms. You don't have to be constantly posting throughout the day just to grab some attention."

"So how do you do it, Phil?"

"Sure, there are people doing some crazy things online that get them a whole lot of followers. But there are lots of other successful authors sharing content that's aligned with their personalities. A lot of authors aren't even on social media and still do well. But this isn't about whether you should be on those platforms. Yeah, they can be helpful for getting free traffic, but I'm talking about the style you use when creating content. It's about whether that content is for these platforms or somewhere else."

"Hell, I don't even know what my style is. Do you have a style, Phil?"

"I do, Marty. I know my style and I didn't need to make a fool of myself for attention. Although if I did, I would've had some fun with it."

"So what did you do to find your style?"

"Marty, you have to remember that you aren't just an author. You're also an entertainer, and there are many ways to be entertaining."

"Like?"

"Tell engaging stories. Pass along something interesting you heard. Reveal your sources of inspiration. Bring readers into your world by showing off your writing space or talking about your routines. These things might be ordinary to you, but they're probably new to your followers. And these are just to name a few."

"You make it sound so easy. Is it?"

"No way! It's tough as hell. A lot of the worthwhile things in life are. Look, Marty, forget about being an instant sensation online and focus on being an engaging entertainer and writer. Find a style that's authentic and make it work for your readers."

"Sound advice, Phil. How did you start?"

"I started finding my niche, short stories, and then progressed to my first novel. Have you got a niche, Marty?" Marty takes a few moments to think before he comes back with a surprising answer.

"You know what, I don't think I have a niche. I guess I need to create one. You've given me a lot of good stuff to think about, Phil. Really. It takes a lot of grit to become a successful author, and after listening to you I think I know what I'll do for my style."

"That's great, Marty. What's your plan?"

"I'm going to do that dancing monkey routine on BookTok and make myself famous."

As I walk out on Marty and his crazy contemporary style, it makes me wonder why writers spend so much time writing, editing, and rewriting when all they have to do is wear a dancing monkey suit.

Doorways

Elizabeth Beckham looks up from her stool at the wall clock: 01:37 AM.

"What am I doing here so late? There's no rush on this project. I could've just gone to Pedro's party or went to bed," she mutters to herself.

Elizabeth lets out an enormous sigh that no one is around to hear. As a horticulturist on Station 747 of Earth's Federation Corporation (EFC), Elizabeth is charged with cultivating plants in gardens in low-gravity space to produce food and medicinal ingredients - not for any comfort or ornamental purposes. The purpose of Elizabeth's work on the space station is to make EFC more money.

Back in the old days, horticulturists were also agriculturists who grow flowers, fruits and nuts, vegetables, and herbs, as well as ornamental trees and lawns. When Elizabeth went to Mars University to study and practice horticulture, she learned that it could be traced back thousands of years.

Horticulture contributed to the transition from nomadic human communities to sedentary, or semi-sedentary, societies.

The practice of horticulture is divided into several categories which focus on the cultivation and processing of different plants and food items for specific purposes. In order to conserve the science of horticulture, multiple organizations worldwide educate, encourage, and promote it. Elizabeth chose to pursue a career in low-gravity horticulture and soon became a highly regarded horticulturist, amongst the likes of Luca Gambino and Luther Berkey.

Now, seeing that it is almost two in the morning, Elizabeth closes up and heads to her room for a good night's sleep. Before she can put away her research, however, she hears a voice.

"Don't go!" Startled, Elizabeth looks around, only to see that she is the only one in the lab. Still, she is certain she heard something. She tells herself that the fatigue is messing with her head.

Taking her lab coat and placing it over her stool, Elizabeth hears the same voice.

"Please stay. Don't go. I need you." Again, she stops to look around, her anxiety mounting. Again, she sees no one. She walks around the lab, just to make sure. Other that the many petri dishes holding seeds and other specimens and some already cultivated plants, she is the only living thing in the lab.

"What is going on?"

"Come closer. Let me feel you closer to me," says the voice. Elizabeth realises then that she is not hearing the voice aloud, but sensing it in her head as if the speaker is contacting her telepathically. Attempting to reach out to whoever is in her head, she thinks:

"Where are you? How do I get closer to you?"

"Here to your right."

Elizabeth looks to her right. There is a counter, and the only thing on it is a woody pear: a tall shrub named for its large, woody, pear-shaped fruit. It grows hard capsules which can reach up to 10cm in length. Each capsule contains two seeds with large papery wings that are released when the fruit splits open. This only occurs when the branches die, often following an Australian bushfire. When this happens, it can take up to three years for a young tree to bear fruit again.

"You mean the woody pear?" asks Elizabeth.

"Yes. It is called the Love Pear in my world, Elizabeth."

"Your world? What do you mean, your world? Who are you and where are you from? How do you know my name?"

"I am called Xylo Melun, and I have been watching you these past few years as you conducted experiments to increase the productivity of your plants in space. I was most fascinated by you, and so I reached out through the Love Pear, which is the only medium through which we can communicate directly with other species not of our dimension. I'm glad I did." Elizabeth takes a seat on the stool with her lab coat draped over it, stunned at this strange conversation that she is having with another being, in another dimension, through an Australian woody pear - the Love Pear, as Xylo calls it. It hardly seems real.

"Pedro, is this you? Are you watching somewhere, waiting for me to do something dumb so you can make me the butt of some joke?"

"That is not the case. Come closer, and I will show you that this is all real." Having nothing to lose and eager to put an end to this charade, Elizabeth gets closer to the woody pear, so close that she can almost sense an aura emitting from it. Suddenly, visions of a strange land fill her mind. It is verdant, luscious, and somehow elicits a rush of excitement.

"Do you feel me now?" Asks Xylo.

Taken aback, Elizabeth has no choice but to accept that this is not Pedro or one of his mates pulling a very elaborate joke. This is really happening. She is in contact with another life form from another dimension.

"I do, Xylo, but how is this possible?"

"Our technology is eons ahead of yours and we have many options for transport, but we find that telepathic communication is the easiest and most cost-effective way to contact other species after we have spent years observing them."

"Oh my goodness. Xylo, I need to get my boss in here right away so you can contact him as well. He'll know how proceed with our diplomatic protocols."

"No. That is not required."

"Not required? What do you mean, not required? We've just made contact for the first time. This is huge, and we need both our governments and species know what's happening."

"No, this is between us only." Elizabeth is surprised by this answer, and can only think to ask:

"What do you mean, between us only?" There is a moment of dead silence, and even in the void of space, that silence can be unbearable. Xylo is the first to break it.

"Elizabeth, you are the top human horticulturist on this station, and you have been navigating these odd waters without knowing that a top alien horticulturist, myself, has been collaborating with you for the past ten years. Have you ever wondered why many of your experiments succeeded after everyone thought they would fail? Have you ever considered how these ideas came to you? I have been helping you along all this time, hoping to find a way to contact you, and your Australian woody pear has proved to be the key."

"OK, so you had a hand in creating this form of contact. Why don't you want our governments to get involved?"

"Simple. I plan to open a doorway between our dimensions so we can visit."

Another surprise; a doorway between dimensions. Will she walk through it, or will Xylo?

"When will you do this, Xylo?"

"Now," is his short answer.

"Now? How do you know it'll work? How do you know you'll survive when the doorway opens? Will I be safe on my side of the doorway? Xylo, I'm not sure we should do this without proper procedures in place by our respective governments."

"Be brave, Elizabeth. I have planned for all contingencies, and everything will be fine. Now do me a favour. Please go to the lab door, lock it, and stand close to it while I open the doorway from my world." In a strange, hypnotic state, Elizabeth does exactly as he says. After locking the lab door, she stands close to it and waits.

Elizabeth senses a vibration through her body and sees the woody pear slowly sway left and right on the counter. As it does so, it emits a small light which grows larger and larger. In less than a minute it engulfs the entire lab counter and reaches throughout the room. Elizabeth can no longer see the woody pear, but she can sense it. Somehow, she knows it is still there.

The light is now so bright that Elizabeth must cover her eyes. Even as she does, however, out of the corners of her vision she sees the brightness diminishing. She lowers her hands from her eyes and sees a figure emerge from the light.

With the door between dimensions opened, she sees her counterpart for the first time. Xylo is tall, green, and resembles a tree, and the strangeness of his appearance leaves her in a state of shock. She can only watch as he steps into the lab and begins to approach.

"Elizabeth, it is so wonderful to see you in the flesh. Here is my Love Pear. I'm ready to inseminate!"

"Your Love Pear? Ready to inseminate? What in the world is going on?" Xylo smiles and laughs, and then launches into his explanation.

"Why Elizabeth, you know what it means. With all the cross fertilisation you have done over the years, we have bonded, and our courtship is over, and we are now ready to proceed to the next level of our relationship."

"This is insane! I didn't even know you existed until tonight, and you think we were courting? Do you really think you can just waltz into my dimension, and we'll immediately have sex?"

"It is what I expected. It seemed like such a good idea."

Without thinking, Elizabeth rushes to the nearest cabinet, grabs a can of Roundup, and sprays Xylo in his face, his body, his arms, everywhere she can point the can to.

Xylo coughs and stumbles towards Elizabeth, who continues to spray him with Roundup. Xylo, helpless before the chemical assault, has no choice but to retreat into the doorway, which immediately closes after his body passes through. Once it does, the lab is left in an eerie silence.

Grabbing the woody pear, Elizabeth heads to the large basin and places it in. She pours Borax, WD-40, and bleach over it and watches as the woody pear shrivels and dies. Even then, she isn't satisfied. She cuts the roots up into tiny pieces and throws them into the furnace, watching as they burn away into ash. Once it's done, Elizabeth takes a seat at her desk and writes her letter of resignation as chief horticulturist of Station 747 for the EFC and requests an immediate transfer to Earth.

She takes the letter, places it on her boss' desk, and turns off the light and leaves the lab. As she storms off, she mutters to herself.

"Across species and dimensions, men really are the same. I'll be damned if I have a plant baby with some guy I just met."

Enthralled

I saw her and stopped in my tracks.

Her blouse made her breasts perk up like meerkats. Her long, flowing hair fell to the back of her arse, landing on what looked like two beautiful scones ready to be devoured. Her ruby red lips seemed to call to me - "take me, take me." Her long arms beckoned - "embrace me, embrace me."

I was enthralled by her beauty and wanted more.

Much more.

I walked over to her.

The next thing I heard was a police officer saying:

"Sir, I don't need a description of the victim. I'm not a sketch artist. I'm the arresting officer, and you're under arrest for improperly disrobing in front of the victim at the Narellan Shopping Centre."

Face

Another freaking Crohn's attack, I think to myself as I lay in the ward at Northport Hospital.

There are four patients in this ward, all men. I introduced myself after they wheeled me in. Interesting characters, the three of them.

First, there's Peter. Peter is a train conductor for Sydney Trains, and he just had an emergency appendectomy. The second patient is a young man who goes by Michael. He's scheduled for a kidney stone procedure and is under some strong pain medication.

Some patients have their curtains drawn specifically; the third patient, who convalesces in the corner bed diagonally across from me, has had his drawn for some time. A mournful cry arises from the occupant, whose name is Hawley Grainger. I think of him as the captain because of his presence and military-style haircut.

"Nurse, nurse," he cries out, his voice low and feeble with age, "the button isn't working."

It's possible he's not pushing it hard enough, but I use mine to summon the nurse, just in case.

When he doesn't get a response to his complaint, he clarifies by pointing to the button that opens the curtain and saying:

"It's not working. You know, the button that opens the curtain." He points to it and again.

"It isn't working."

Interesting.

My curtains don't have a button to operate them. The only way to draw the curtains, thanks to a defect in their design, is to wrestle them along their runners. Everyone - patients, visitors, even nurses - struggles for minutes on end to draw or un-draw them.

A nurse arrives, and I point to the captain. The nurse shrugs her shoulders, comes behind my bed and turns off my buzzer, and heads over to my ward companion.

"The button that opens the curtain isn't working," the captain repeats.

“There isn’t a button to open the curtains,” she replies, and begins manually yanking the curtain open, revealing the captain within, sitting fully dressed on the side of his bed. As he observes her in the laborious process of pulling the curtain back, he seems to ponder this revelation. Then, something more urgent than the curtains strikes him.

“Nurse, I wonder whether you could help me with a rather embarrassing issue.” The captain is unfailingly polite.

“What is it, love?” Nurses routinely use the most intimate expressions of endearment to address us. I’ve never felt as much of a “love” or a “darling” as I have during my time here.

“It’s my teeth. I’ve looked everywhere for them. They seem to have disappeared,” the captain says. He lowers his voice a little.

“Your teeth.”

“I had them at breakfast, but there’s no sign of them now.” The captain is fretting, a touch cantankerous now. The nurse checks his nightstand.

“I’ve looked everywhere,” he wails. She turns to look at him and her mouth twitches.

"Mr Grainger," she says, "your teeth are in your mouth."

"In my mouth? Are you sure?"

"Yes. I can see them, Mr Grainger."

"Nurse, can you check, please? I cannot feel them."

The nurse leans down to Mr Grainger and starts feeling his face.

"Please open your mouth, Mr Grainger." The captain does as he is told, and the nurse takes his hand and places it in his mouth.

"See. Can't you feel them?" He runs his fingers over them and his eyes widen in realization.

"Oh, my goodness, so they are! I am so dreadfully, dreadfully sorry."

"Not to worry, Mr Grainger. I'm pleased we found them," she says.

"So am I."

As the nurse leaves, I see that the captain has a big grin on his face. Once she is out of ear short, he looks at me and says:

"Nice to be touched by a lady."

"So you knew you had your teeth in?"

“Oh yes, I did. I just wanted to feel her soft hands on my face. I miss the touch of a woman, and since my wife Mary passed away three years ago, I seek it out however I can.”

“My, you're a cheeky one.”

“No son, just in need of human touch…” and he falls asleep in the middle of our conversation. Left with only my thoughts, I ruminate on the loneliness that drives this man to trick into nurses touching him. Touch is something we take for granted. We can't live without it, and yet we don't realize that simple fact until we reach out and no one is there.

The sound of footsteps on the linoleum floor jars me from my thoughts. I turn and see my wife, Miriam, enter the ward.

“Hi sweetie, how are you today?”

“Missing you. Touch my face. I need to feel your hands,” I reply, holding out my hand.

Gerry's New Girlfriend

Once upon a time, there was a young man by the name of Gerald Pembrooke - Gerry, to his few friends. Gerry was not very good at expressing his feelings. He kept them inside, and as a result, people often misunderstood him.

In school, he sat behind a girl, and he grew to like her. One day, he worked up the courage to ask her for a date. He quickly flubbed the speech he had rehearsed so many times in preparation of this moment, and the girl walked away, laughing loudly to herself.

When Gerry went to school dances, he would try to hang out with the other dateless boys. They pushed him aside, keeping him on the outside of their groups. Even the geeks did not let him into their conversations.

Sadie Hawkins dances were completely out of the question; no girl ever asked him to go. So the years went by, and eventually he was a junior in high school who had never had a girlfriend.

He felt so alone.

One night, Gerry was lying in bed, feeling miserable, when suddenly he heard a strange noise. As he looked around the room, he saw a pink apparition hovering in the corner. The apparition seemed to look right at him, and it smiled. The thing seemed to float a foot off the bedroom floor and it moved gradually through the air, closer and closer to Gerry.

He was, for a moment, scared, but he was also curious. As it came even closer, Gerry could see it was a girl. Or at least, it looked like a girl. With that revelation, he became even more interested in finding out more about it. He asked the apparition what it wanted. She gave a simple reply.

"I want to be your girlfriend." This bold statement took him aback, not least because he had never heard these words even from a flesh-and-blood human. He wasn't sure what to say.

"I…I don't know," he stammered. "I've never been in a relationship with a ghost before." The apparition smiled.

"That's alright," she said. "I am new to this, too." This gave him a little more confidence, and he decided to see where it went.

"Do you have a name?"

"Yes, I do. Belinda." To Gerry, that seemed the loveliest name in the world.

"Belinda, how long have you been an apparition?"

"I do not know. Last thing I remember was I was strolling on Fournier Street in London, and I heard some screaming and someone shouting *grab the horses*. Then there was just darkness, and I have been here ever since. By the way, where am I?" What a story! It was now Gerry's turn to answer questions.

"You're in my bedroom in Northport, New South Wales, Australia. Do you know where that is?"

"No," Belinda said with a smile.

Gerry and the apparition talked for a while longer. They learned about each other's lives, and their hopes and dreams. Gerry found himself drawn to the apparition's kind nature and gentle flowing. She was different from any girl he had ever met.

In the end, Gerry decided he had nothing to lose and gave the relationship a try.

He and Belinda started dating.

Gerry took Belinda on many dates.

He took her to the grocery store.

They visited the petrol station to fill up his automobile. Belinda said that was the manliest thing she had ever seen Gerry do.

A trip to the Northport Observatory, operated by the Down Under Society, was so much a thrill that Belinda, for a moment, vanished into thin air. She soon popped up again, eager to continue the tour.

They were happy together, and they did not care what anyone thought.

No one could see Belinda for some unexplained reason, which presented challenges to their relationship.

Sometimes Gerry would be seen talking into thin air, and people would make sure they avoided him or the table next to him if he and Belinda were at a restaurant.

Waiters would scratch their heads when Gerry ordered two meals, no one showed up, and he paid for both, leaving one plate empty and the other untouched.

Gerry was happy, but he still felt that something was off. He longed to touch Belinda and share physical intimacy with her. Yet even without a corporeal form, Belinda was always there for him, and she always made him feel loved.

Years went by, they fell deep in love, and Gerry proposed to her.

"How are we going to do this? We are of two different worlds!" Belinda asked him in surprise.

"Don't worry, my love. I got this," is all he said to her.

Gerry told his parents and his very few friends about the wedding, and even got a celebrant to do the honours in his parents' home. He was, for the first time in his life, truly happy. Not even her incorporeal nature could sour their special day.

The wedding was to be small and unpretentious. He did not bother with a tuxedo but did splurge on a new suit from "Tuxedos R Us." When the day came, he looked simply magnificent.

With his family and few friends looking on, Gerry stood in front of the divan in his parents' lounge area and nodded to the musician he hired to play the wedding march on his ukelele. When the first note rang out, Belinda entered the room and slowly floated towards Gerry in her best pinkish glow.

Everyone looked at Gerry in astonishment, for he wore the biggest smile they had ever seen.

He was happy.

Belinda arrived and floated next to Gerry, and he nodded to the celebrant to start.

You could see the celebrant was confused. He was told what to expect, but it still rattled him. Nevertheless, for $500 he did as he was told and started the ceremony.

After a few minutes, he asked the important question.

"Do you, Belinda, take Gerry as your husband?" He stared at the empty space across from Gerry.

Belinda looked at Gerry, smiled and said:

"Yes."

Gerry turned to the small group gathered, and excitedly relayed the happy news.

"She said yes!" His parents smiled and one of his friends let out a small giggle, but the ceremony continued.

"Gerry, do you take Belinda as your wife?"

"Yes, I do," was his answer.

Looking at Gerry, the small group of attendees, and at the spot where Belinda was floating, the celebrant proclaimed:

"I pronounce you husband and wife. You may now kiss the bride." This incited quite the commotion from the few attendees, but this was nothing compared to what Gerry did next.

"Mum, dad, friends. I know you can't see my beautiful Belinda, but she's real. I know she's real. So real that I'm going to join her." With that, Gerry pulled a .38 pistol from his new suit and blew his brains out.

When the police arrived and took everyone's statements, they ruled it as a suicide. Gerry and Belinda, however, thought it had been a beautiful ceremony, and together they lived happily ever after.

Hell's Bells

Lucinda looks around the room and sighs.

"Where in hell's bells is that darn husband of mine?" She says as she places the final lunch plate on the table.

"All he had to do was help old man Angus put Big Boy on the trailer to get him to market. This shouldn't have taken over thirty minutes. What's keeping him?"

Lucinda goes to the front door and lets out a loud call, telling Oscar to get in for lunch.

She hears no reply.

The only thing left to do is go out onto the station and look for him. By the time she finishes scouring it for any sign of Oscar, it is past midday. He is not to be found.

"Where in hell's bells is that man?" She mutters to herself.

Lucinda yells out Oscar's name several more times around the barn and the nearby paddocks. He does not reply.

As she comes up on the main paddock, she sees that Big Boy is not in it, and she can't hear the red bell that rings incessantly as it dangles around the neck of the 185 centimetre-tall bull. Maybe Oscar got Big Boy into the trailer after all, and off to the market station he had gone.

"Yes, that has to be it," she says, and heads back home to have her lunch. Oscar can warm up his when he gets back.

After several hours with no sign of her husband, Lucinda begins to worry. She grabs her keys, gets into the old Ford Ute, and drives down the road to trace Oscar's trip into town.

She does not have to drive far. She soon spots Oscar's tractor and the trailer containing Big Boy on the side of the road. Her husband is lying motionless on the roadway. She brings the Ute to a screeching halt and practically stumbles out the door as she rushes to her husband. She is too late; Oscar is dead.

Kneeling next to his lifeless body, all she can think is:

How did this happen?

Picking up her phone, she calls Angus, her nearest neighbour, and the local police station.

In tears, with sobs wracking her body, she kneels next to Oscar and waits for them to come. Angus soon arrives, and a few minutes later, the local constabulary, Peter, gets to the scene as well.

Looking at the holes in Oscar's chest, which could only have been caused by a pair of horns, and the distance he lay from the trailer, Lucinda's first thought is that Big Boy got riled up and Oscar tried to calm him down. Instead, he got charged and was sent flying, and his head hit on the road. This is what she tells Peter as Angus holds her close, his arms wrapped tight around her.

After she gives her account to the Constable, Sargent Greg McKinley arrives and looks over the scene. He kneels over Oscar's body and studies it for a few minutes. McKinley takes a pen from his pocket and touches Oscar's hands, inspecting them more closely. Then he looks over Oscar's upper body and his neck. Finally, he goes over to the trailer and sees Big Boy restlessly pacing inside. The bull is unharmed but seems to be focused on the grisly scene outside.

McKinley then walks over to where Lucinda is standing with Angus' arms around her and asks her to repeat her story. As she does so, the Sargent's eyes flit from her to Angus. When she finishes, he turns to her neighbour.

"Well Angus, what's your side of the story?"

"Well, Sarge, I was up at the Brompton's when Oscar called me to help him load up Big Boy. I did, and then we rode off. We stopped for a bit at my place, and then he kept going while I stayed there. I didn't know anything had happened until Lucinda here called."

"How did you get those red stains on your hands, Angus?" Asks McKinley. Angus looks at his hands and stares at the stains as if seeing them for the first time. He can't answer the question, which prompts McKinley to gesture for the constable to approach.

"Angus Flemington, I am arresting you on suspicion of the murder of Oscar Brompton," McKinley says. Lucinda, horrified at this proclamation, screams in protest.

"No, you got it all wrong, Sargent! Angus would never have hurt Oscar!" Argus' protests joined hers, but Constable Peter puts his arms behind him and cuffs him after reading him his rights. He then leads Angus to his patrol car, pressing his head down beneath the roof as he pushes Angus into the backseat.

McKinley comes over to Lucinda to calm her down, and when she does, he shares something with her.

"Lucinda, you and Angus were having an affair. Am I right?" Lucinda is stunned by the declaration but does not refute it.

"Somewhere along the trip, Oscar confronted Angus about the affair and stopped the truck and trailer. Both men got out. Sensing something, Big Boy got rattled and started bucking a bit. Both men stopped their argument to settle the bull, but Angus got an idea. He grabbed Big Boy's red bell and yanked it as hard as he could while pushing Oscar into the bull. Big Boy reacted as a normal bull would and lunged at him, sending him flying over the trailer onto the road. His skull hit the pavement and he died instantly."

"How? Why? How can you tell that happened?"

"That's what everything I've seen here today leads me to believe, and Angus will come around and confess the details. Those stains on his hands gave it away. Your husband has the exact same ones. They're from that rusted bell around Big Boy's neck."

"So, it wasn't an accident, Sargent McKinley?" Lucinda asks meekly.

"No. Angus wanted to make it look like Big Boy killed Oscar in a freak accident, but it was his actions that caused your husband's death. It's murder, all right."

"How did you suspect that Angus and I were in an affair?"

"He couldn't keep his hands off you, even with your husband's corpse right at his feet."

"I wasn't involved in my husband's death. You've got to believe me."

"I know you weren't, but if not for your affair, he might still be here. That's something you'll have to live with. Now go home. Come to the station tomorrow and make a statement. I'll call in Jefferson's Auction House to come and pick up Big Boy."

Lucinda gets back into her Ute and drives home, wondering how it was so easy for McKinley to figure out she was having an affair.

"Hell's bells," was all she could say.

Hidden in Plain Sight

She had kept them for years, tucked away in a box that was left amongst the other old shoe boxes high in her closet. They were letters from a man she had once loved, and although the years had passed, his words were still as vivid and real as if he had written them yesterday. They were cherished memories to be lived through again and again.

She read through them, feeling the emotions of the past wash over her. His promises of love all sounded familiar, and yet she couldn't remember exactly when he had penned his thoughts to paper.

He had been a part of her life long ago, and yet his words in ink were still enough to make her heart ache.

Was she still in love with him?

She thought her feelings had faded a long time ago, but now she wasn't so sure. She had kept the letters, after all, and they rekindled the flame she thought that time had snuffed out.

Where was he?

Did he advance his career as he had hoped?

Were his disapproving parents still alive?

Did he move away, or did he still live in the old mansion?

She never went by the mansion, fearing she would see him there and that the sight of him would hurt too much, but now she was gripped by a desire to get answers to her questions.

Did she dare visit?

Slowly, she refolded the letters and placed them back in the old box. As she gently rested it back in that hiding area in plain sight, she took satisfaction in knowing that his words, at least, would always be there with her.

Ready for her if she felt lonely again.

Invasion

Matial towers triumphant over the dead bodies of his two challengers in the killing circle. Blood slowly dripping from his spear, he stands in front of his father-king, Itzcoatl, and waits for him to acknowledge his victory.

King Itzcoatl looks at his son and smiles.

At the youthful age of twenty-two, Matial has proven himself to be stronger, faster, and a more skillful warrior than anyone in his kingdom. Yet King Itzcoatl is irked by his son's arrogance. Matial thinks too highly of himself.

The king has a plan to bring his son down to earth, so that he may rule without his head in the clouds when Itzcoatl is no longer able. He had received word from the coast that a boat had landed, manned by small people. Their leader, whose face none had seen, was said to be even more diminutive than the rest of the crew. They were friendly and wished to make trade arrangements, but during the discussions a misunderstanding led to an altercation, and the strangers were all gathered up and brought to the palace for Itzcoatl to decide what to do with them.

Itzcoatl is a wise man. He understands the benefit of further trade opportunities and made it a point to find out from witnesses what had happened. By all accounts, it was his own emissary's fault, for he made the perilous error which cost him his life. It was not the fault of the newcomers. The king had heard that they fight in very peculiar ways, and it occurred to him that he could make use of their martial prowess to humble his son while repairing relations with the new arrivals.

"Well done, my son. You have made me proud and continue to earn your warriors' respect with your prowess," says Itzcoatl.

"Thank you, my King. I serve at your pleasure."

"I need you to rest for tomorrow, my son. I have a new challenge for you."

"What is this challenge, my king?"

"Strangers have landed on our shore, and they have taken a life, but I have decided that instead of an execution, I would like you to challenge their leader."

"I will slay him before your eyes, my king."

"No. You will spill no blood. You will fight only with your hands and body, to show our people your prowess even without weapons." Matial considers this. No blood? Where is the fun in that? Perhaps his father has gone soft. Or, perhaps, there is a purpose in showing his strength without a lance. It might make him look even more fearsome before his subjects.

"Yes, my king. I accept this challenge, and I will defeat this stranger for you." King Itzcoatl nods and Matial leaves the killing circle to clean up, refresh himself, and prepare for his upcoming battle with the stranger.

Overnight, the exciting news of a new match spreads amongst the populace and the prospect of seeing Matial fight without weapons makes the betting even more frenzied. The crowd is expected to be massive, larger than any that gathered for Matial's previous matches.

The morning finds Matial refreshed and jubilant, for once again he is to prove his worth to his father and his subjects.

Taking one last swig of pulque, he heads to the killing circle for his fight. Wearing the royal loincloth and overgarment, he cuts an impressive figure. He stands at 173 centimetres, very tall for his people. His size is highly revered, and it has proved valuable in all his challenges.

Matial arrives to great cheers and sees his father sitting on his throne. He offers his father a deep bow. The king acknowledges the bow and Matial proceeds to the centre of the circle, where he takes off his overgarment and hands it to a servant boy, who rushes off.

Matial sighs as he waits. He misses his lance, but he will do what he must for his father.

When his opponent enters the killing circle, Matial cannot help but smile. The stranger is a runt. He cannot be over 150 centimetres tall. Matial lets confidence flow through him; he is certain this will be an easy fight.

His opponent wears a black, skin-tight outfit covering his entire body, with a scarf of some sort hiding his mouth and hair. The only parts of him Matial can see are the stranger's deep brown eyes and small, pale hands. He has never seen such clothes before, but they do nothing to dampen his self-assurance. He will finish this battle quickly and then head off on a new adventure with his friends in court.

King Itzcoatl gives the order to begin, and the spectators go wild.

Overconfident, Matial rushes the stranger who casually sidesteps and trips him, causing Matial to fall flat on his face. The impact kicks up dust and elicits a ripple of laughter from the crowd.

Embarrassed by his fall, Matial gets up and studies his opponent with newfound caution. His size makes him quick, and Matial realizes that he must be more alert to the challenger's movements. He ponders whether the stranger will employ some other unorthodox tactic.

The stranger does not move. He stands perfectly still, waiting for Matial to act. This infuriates Matial, who abandons alertness and instead rushes his small foe in a rage.

As he charges, the smaller man crouches down and hold both hands in front of his body, curling his fingers to resemble the sharp-clawed paws of a cougar. When Matial goes to grab him, he takes Matial's left hand and flips him over, causing him to land once again on the dirt. Dust and laughter from the crowd both fill the air. Their laughs are growing louder and more rambunctious, having seen him humiliated a second time.

Matial gets up and looks at his adversary with hate pouring from his heart.

The stranger now stands in a very particular way.

He balances on one leg, like a flamingo, and has his arms extended perpendicular to his sides. It looks as if he is ready to fly, with one leg in front of him suspended in the air.

He is still as a statue, balanced, in form, and in control. Again, he waits for Matial to act.

Matial thinks it may be best to inch his way towards his opponent, and he does so. Matial approaches slowly, getting closer and closer.

His enemy does not move.

He just continues to wait.

When Matial gets within reach, and before he can make a move, the stranger leaps into the air. Bringing up the leg that had remained on the ground for balance, he lands a kick to Matial's jaw.

Matial falls back hard and does not immediately rise to his feet.

The stunt makes the crowd go quiet.

He lies there for a moment and runs a hand over his sore jaw. Not broken, but it will hurt for a while.

As he remains lying in the dirt, the stranger approaches him. He stands next to Matial and extends his hand as if to offer him assistance in rising.

Matial accepts the gesture, but it is only a feint. He grabs his smaller foe and wrestles him to the ground. In the tussle, the scarf comes off and Matial freezes.

It is not a man, but a woman he has been fighting.

Shocked by this, Matial loses his grip, and the woman quickly unravels herself from his grasp and stands, looking down at Matial.

She has an oval-shaped face, pointed, narrow chin, and plump lips that are pursed into the shape of a warrior's bow. He is struck by her beauty.

Matial looks at the crowd and then at his father.

Silence.

He needs to win. As he prepares to lunge at his opponent, she bends at the waist and gives a deep bow to Matial, showing him respect as a higher status individual.

Matial stops in his tracks. She has conceded. Why?

From behind him, King Itzcoatl proclaims:

"The challenge is complete. My son has unmasked the stranger. A worthy opponent, and one who will not suffer for any past indiscretions. Let us now congratulate both warriors for this magnificent display of fighting prowess." Itzcoatl claps, and the crowd joins in.

Standing in the killing circle, Matial looks at the small woman and wonders to himself:

If the women fight like this, what would happen if the men invaded?

Kung Pao My Heart

Detective Pierre Jackson was on his way to his favourite restaurant for a quick meal when a car hit him as he crossed the road. A bystander called for an ambulance, which arrived on the scene and transported Detective Jackson to the hospital. The emergency room staff treated his broken leg, and then they placed him in a room to be monitored. Still hankering for his favourite meal, he calls the restaurant from his hospital bed.

"Hello, this is *Wok Do You Want*, this is Mei. Take order please," says the young woman who answers the phone.

"Mei, Jackson here. I need a delivery of my favourite, please."

"Ah, Detective Jackson, you want Kung Pao My Heart delivered to your house or the station, yes?"

"Not this time, Mei. Can you deliver it to General Hospital, Level 7, Ward 2, Room 20 as soon as you can? I'm starved."

"Hospital? Oh, Detective Jackson, you alright? What happened?" Asks Mei, her neutral order-taking tone replaced by one of concern.

Jackson explains what happened and finishes the conversation with a renewed plea for his favourite meal.

"Hurry Mei, I am dwindling away to the size of a warehouse."

"Oh, Detective, you are always so funny. I will get Qián Duōduō to deliver the Kung Pao My Heart. I tell the chef to make the spicy chicken extra hot so it heats things up for while in the hospital." With a laugh, Mei hangs up.

While waiting for his meal to be delivered, Pierre uses his time to resolve the murder case he was working on before the accident.

The victim was a young woman who had been found strangled in her apartment. Jackson had interviewed her friends and family, but no one seemed to know who would want to hurt her. He thought they would never solve the case.

But then, he had an idea. He asked his colleagues to get him a copy of the security footage from the night of the murder and email it to him. He watched the footage repeatedly, and finally, he saw something that no one else had noticed.

In the footage, he saw a man lurking in the shadows outside of the victim's apartment building. The man was wearing a hoodie and a cap, so Jackson couldn't get a good look at his face, but he is sure that man is the killer. And Jackson knows who he is.

Pierre calls a number on his mobile, gives a few quick commands, and waits for his food to arrive.

Twenty-five minutes later, in comes Qián Duōduō with his delivery of Kung Pao My Heart.

"Detective Jackson, Mei told chef to make it boiling like you like, OK?"

"That is correct Qián Duōduō. Hot is how I like it. How much do I owe?"

"$19.80 plus delivery of $2 and of course tip for Qián Duōduō," a smiling Qián Duōduō declares.

Handing Qián Duōduō a twenty and a five note, Pierre says:

"Here, keep the change. By the way, I have another tip for you as well. Want to know what it is?"

"Yes Detective, of course. What is tip?"

"Never wear your work clothes to do a murder."

Qián Duōduō's eyes go wide in shock. Before he can answer, three burly officers walk into the room, place him under arrest, and read him his rights.

Qián Duōduō confesses to the murder on the spot, and is taken away. Pierre is proud of himself for solving the case while stuck in the hospital. He knows that the victim's family will be grateful for his work, and that they will at last have closure.

As Qián Duōduō is dragged from the room, Pierre opens his delivery box and starts munching on his Kung Pao My Heart.

"Finally, my favourite."

Loudmouth

Felicity waits for Mary to speak. Mary does not, and eventually, she loses her patience.

"Well. Are you going to say something, or should I?"

"It's a bit tricky with the loudmouth millennials next to us shouting at the top of their lungs."

Sarah nods vigorously and chimes in.

"I can hardly hear a word Beatrice is saying over their racket!"

"What did you say, Sarah? I couldn't hear," I say loudly.

The monthly meeting of the Australian Publishing Consortium had convened at our local haunt: the White Sheep Hotel, in beautiful Northport, New South Wales. At least, it was supposed to. Instead, a group of inconsiderate young people are drowning out every other word, keeping us from getting to anything on our agenda.

"Felicity, were you or Mary going to say something?" Asks Agnes. She is the group's most prolific author, with six self-published books under her belt.

"I agreed with Sarah and Mary. It's too damn loud," says Arthur, who rarely attends meetings but has chosen today to show up. Now, he encourages the admonitions of the troublemakers at the table next to us.

"Look at them. No consideration for other patrons of this establishment. Loudmouth millennial hoodlums. That's what you called them, right Agnes?"

"I did not call them loudmouth millennial hoodlums, though that is an excellent description. If I had to assign them a label, it would be something like pests, troublemakers, or even rabble-rousers. They think they own the place, thoroughly drowning out any other attempts at conversation with their noisy nonsense."

"Now Agnes, we must admit that we were just as rowdy at that age, if not worse. Perhaps we just let them have their fun and speak even louder," I interject.

"Everyone, I've heard enough," announces Felicity, her voice carrying over the din.

"As the group's moderator, I feel I should be the one to go over there and confront the noisy group and ask them to tone it down. I will be right back." Felicity walks over to the other table, stands above the young people, and in an authoritative voice says:

"Ladies and gentlemen, we are a group of authors trying to conduct a meeting at the table next to you. You have been excessively loud since we came in, and we have had a terrible time carrying on a conversation. Can you tone it down some so we can talk?"

In the wake of Felicity's proclamation, silence hangs between the millennial table and that of the Australian Publishing Consortium. Then, a girl who could not have been older than nineteen stands up, looks at our table, and addressed Felicity.

"Miss, we had to raise our voices because your table's been really loud ever since we walked in. We were just trying to hear each other over all the noise you were making. So maybe your table's the one that should tone it down."

We are in total shock. It turns out the real loudmouths were us!

Morning Headlines

"Bob, don't you just love this library?" Peter asks, admiring his surroundings. Bob stretches his arms and arches his back in a long stretch as he looks around the library.

According to the history of the University of Sydney, the university received thirty thousand pounds from the estate of the late Thomas Fisher, a retired bootmaker and property investor, to be used in establishing and maintaining a library.

After receiving the funds, it took some time for the university to decide how best to carry out the estate's wishes. The Chancellor thought they should use the funds to erect a building and contribute to the salary of a librarian, but the Vice Chancellor and Library Committee wanted to put the money towards books. In 1887, they reached a compromise. It was decided that over twenty-thousand pounds accumulated interest would be set aside for a building fund, in hopes that the government would provide matching funding, and the balance of ten-thousand pounds would be directed to an endowment for books.

Eight years later, under architect Walter Vernon and with support from the government of New South Wales, construction on the building began. It took eight years to complete.

Many generations had passed, and now Bob sits within the copper-clad outer walls of Fisher South or building F04. It is an accessible stack library with a vast historical collection. The building also houses the East Asia collection and the University Archives and has some silent study desks and larger tables to fit large groups of students. A few students from the School of Psychology now sit around them, huddling and speaking in hushed tones.

Bob does not respond to Peter's remark about the library; he hardly even hears it. He is more focused on the books within the library than the building itself. In his fourth-year honours program, he is less concerned with architecture than with his 18,000-to-20,000-word thesis due next week.

"You okay?" Peter asks. A small frown forms on Bob's face as he works, and he briefly turns to Peter.

"Not really. I got a promising idea and an outline, but I'm missing something. What's the word I'm looking for? Oh, yeah, inspiration." Peter looks over Bob's shoulder, smiles and leans closer to him.

"Look to your right. I believe she just walked in!" He whispers. Bob turns to look, and once he does, he cannot look away.

Walking in, holding two books in her arms, is a tall, lovely Japanese woman. Bob takes in her wide, pale face and large eyes, which are angled slightly downwards. He has never seen a woman with such rich amber irises, and her eyes are all the more mesmerizing for their uniqueness. She is wearing light blue jeans with a V-neck white blouse. Her jumper, a darker, ocean blue, blends just perfectly with her skin. Strapped to her back is a Japanese biwa lute. Bob takes notice of this and finds it strange, but it is far less intriguing than the woman carrying it. He puts the thought out of his mind.

"Wow, you're right Peter. Quite an inspiration. I wonder who she is. I haven't seen her before, have you?"

"No. Transfer student, maybe?"

"Oh crap. She's coming right for us. Quick, stop looking at her. Act normal," Bob hisses, despite continuing to stare himself.

"You're the one gawking."

When she reaches their table, the woman stops, smiles, and asks in fluent English:

"Hi, can I join you?"

"Of course. I'm Bob and this is my friend, Peter."

"Hello, my name is Juna Jorô…" She murmurs the last bit, and it is too quiet for Bob to hear.

"My friends just call me JJ. It's nice to meet you," she says at normal volume.

"Welcome, JJ. We haven't seen you before. Did you just transfer here?" Placing her books and biwa on the table, JJ sits and gives out a gigantic sigh.

"Boy, I'm tired today. And there's still so much research left for my thesis. How about you guys?"

"Same here JJ," says Bob. "I'm working on my outline right now, but I'm a little stumped on which way to go. What are you working on?"

"Oh, nothing important. Let's talk about something else. No more studying!" JJ says, giggling a little. Bob and Peter exchange glances and shrug their shoulders. Why not? They have had enough late-night studying anyway.

"Sure JJ. What do you want to talk about?"

"Are you hot? I'm feeling flushed." JJ gets up and takes off her jumper, revealing her bare arms. As she leans back to place the jumper over the chair, both Peter and Bob notice a tattoo on her neck. It seems to be a long, pointed appendage, like a thin leg. They cannot tell for sure, and they have little time to stare as JJ quickly turns back to face them.

"No, I'm OK," says Peter. Bob just stares at JJ. She is so lovely. He knows he has to say something, anything, to avoid looking stupid. He needs to impress her.

"JJ, I notice you have a biwa. Do you play the lute?"

"I have played the biwa for many years, and I am exceptionally good at gagaku. Do you know what that is?"

"Of course. Gagaku is ancient Japanese court music. Though most gagaku music is of foreign origin, imported from China and Korea as early as the sixth century and established as a court tradition in Japan by the eighth century."

"Goodness, you know your stuff," JJ says admiringly, letting out one of those lovely giggles of hers.

"Well, I am doing my thesis on ancient Asian studies, so I better know what I'm writing about."

"Hey man, I hate to be a party-pooper here, but I'm getting hungry, so I'm going to split and grab some food. You want to come?" Asks Peter. Before Bob can answer, JJ grabs his hands, leans closer to him, and whispers into his ear.

"Let him go by himself. Let's stay and talk longer, OK?"

"You go Peter. JJ and I will stay a bit longer."

"OK, you two. Behave," Peter says as he gathers his books and leaves. Left alone with JJ, Bob continues staring at her, utterly entranced. JJ looks around the library. It is now empty. She glances at her watch; the time is 9:40 PM.

"We're alone now, Bob. How about I find a secluded corner and play the biwa for you? Would you like that?" Surprised at JJ's invitation, Bob merely nods as she gets up, grabs the biwa, and heads off to find an isolated spot.

Bob sits for a moment and wonders where this is going. She is sending strong signals, and yet JJ is quite an attractive woman. She is clearly out of his league, and yet she approached him and very obviously wanted to be with him alone. Maybe she is just a nice, if rather forward, person. He tries to keep his mind from wandering elsewhere.

Remember Occam's Razor. Go with the simplest explanation.

A moment later, Bob hears the soft, rich, percussive sounds of wood striking the biwa's silk strings, and the distinctive buzzing produced by the strings pressing against the hard wood of the neck. JJ has found a spot and is summoning him.

Checking again, he sees that the few students from before have indeed left, and then he goes looking for JJ. As Bob winds between tables and bookcases, he finds the semi-dark area from which the gentle buzzing is emanating. He heads towards it.

Reaching the sound, Bob can sense JJ's presence but cannot see her in the darkness. She must be there, for the lute continues to play.

"JJ, are you here? I can't see you?"

"I'm here Bob. Come closer."

Bob keeps walking towards the music, lured by its sound, a sound that urges him to her as if by magic. What is happening?

"JJ?"

The sound from the lute stops, and Bob feels JJ standing beside him.

"JJ. What's going on?"

In a moment, JJ grabs Bob's hand and allows herself to be touched. A thrill runs through him like a shiver. She is smooth, her skin soft and cold. He realizes he is feeling her breasts, but before he can stop himself, arms envelop him. There are far more than two, and they hold him so tight that he cannot move.

"What the hell…"

He looks straight at JJ and does not see a woman. Instead, he is embraced by a spider.

His mind races.

JJ introduced herself as Juna Jorô something or other, but she was mumbling. Did she mean to say Jorôgumo, the legendary spider-woman of Japanese mythology who would lure men to her and devour them?

As JJ's multiple arms disrobe him, Bob realises he might not be finishing his thesis. Before the Jorôgumo's work is done, he has one final thought.

I wonder what the headlines will be in the morning.

Murder on the Jezioro Express

It is five minutes to midnight, and Elsa Dubois is racing down the platform to catch the 12:01 AM Jezioro Express, departing from Schiaparelli Central on its weekly circumnavigating luxury Mars tour.

Elsa has saved two years' worth of annual bonuses for this trip, and she will not miss the train.

Elsa stops for a moment and takes off her Jaime Taliento high heels. The price for them was another year's bonus.

These damn things are killing my feet…but they look so good on me.

With her high heels in her left hand, she raises her right to the conductor in the hopes it sees her and does not let the Express take off without her.

"Thank you for holding the train. I thought I was going to miss it," Elsa says as she reaches the conductor.

"Miss, the Jezioro Express will leave in two minutes. I did not hold it for you," it replies as it takes her boarding ticket. It takes a moment to read the code printed on it, and once it is satisfied of the ticket's validity, it addresses her again.

"Welcome Miss Dubois. I am RRC-101, your trip conductor. Please proceed to carriage number seven, room three. Breakfast tomorrow will start at 6 AM promptly, and goes on until 9 AM." Elsa takes her boarding ticket and, without acknowledging RRC-101, boards the first carriage as instructed.

It didn't need to sound so rude. They should do a better job programming etiquette into the robots. Perhaps I'll write a review on it when I finish my holiday.

Elsa lingered on the robot's lack of decorum as she headed to her compartment. So far, the Jezioro Express was not impressing her, but the travel agent had praised it so effusively that she could not help but experience the journey herself:

The Jezioro Express is the crème de la crème of Mars travel. Yes, you can go from one dome city to another in a few hours in a hover-flyer, but where's the fun in that? The Jezioro Express presents the traveler with a luxury no longer found, not even on Earth. Filled with old-time elegance and charm and regarded as one of the greatest train journeys of all time, The Jezioro Express delivers so much more than an extended train ride. It promises access to parts of Mars no other holiday can. The perfect balance of comfort and adventure, culminating in an experience that will move you in every sense of the word.

This was hardly the only draw. Elsa had also been intrigued by the exclusivity of the journey aboard the Jezioro Express.

The Express comprised the locomotive, the executive carriage (really a combination kitchen/storage/crew quarters all-in-one), the restaurant/bar carriage, then the lounge/bar carriage, and finally the three travelers' carriages comprising the platinum class, the premium class, and the gold class, each with three rooms. Each class had its own amenities and, of course, its own price level.

While the Jezioro Express accommodation carriages essentially divided passengers based on their status in society, the restaurant and lounge carriages brought everyone into the same place. Everyone ate and socialised together.

The scenery, of course, was a draw of its own. Seen from the Express, the Red Planet was beautiful. There were some truly magnificent craters along the journey, as well as a bird's-eye view of the cities that had arisen in the wake of humanity's colonisation of Mars. There were also activities planned at an event stop, about which Elsa had heard marvellous things.

But the attraction that ultimately convinced Elsa to spend her hard-earned money was the prospect of relaxing on the Jezioro Express as it circumnavigated the planet in one hundred eighty-nine hours and twenty-eight minutes.

Two years' worth of bonus pay later, she had enough to book a trip in gold class. She is one of nine individuals onboard who are making this one-of-a-kind journey.

She cannot wait.

Elsa still holds her shoes in her left hand and has her carry-on bag slung over her right shoulder as she steps into the first carriage: the restaurant carriage. She looks around, marveling at the exquisite China already set up for breakfast.

Walking through into the lounge, she finds another robot tending the bar and two gentlemen in conversation who, upon seeing her, stop. One nods at Elsa and the other stands and introduces himself, grabbing her left hand holding her shoes.

"Good evening, Miss. Welcome aboard. My name is Vince Cappelli," he says, leaning down and kissing the back of her hand. Elsa blushes a little and is about to introduce herself when Cappelli nods towards the other man.

"This is my brother and business partner, Mr Dino Cappelli. I hope to see more of you during the trip."

"My pleasure, gentlemen. My name is Elsa Dubois. I wish I could stay and chat, but I'm quite tired and would like to retire. We have an exciting trip ahead of us, and I'm certain we'll be seeing more of each other. Goodnight, sirs."

"Goodnight, Miss Dubois. Please call me Vince."

"Alright then, Vince it is. Goodnight," Elsa responds with a smile. She continues towards the gold carriage, thinking she now only had six more passengers to meet tomorrow morning.

As she moves into the platinum carriage, Elsa hears the occupant of room one snoring like a walrus, but both rooms two and three are quiet. Moving on through the premium carriage, room one is silent, but she hears a couple of female voices in room two giggling. Elsa cannot help herself; she stops to listen. Their words are indiscernible behind the door, but Elsa hears the giggling continue until suddenly it halts.

Stop being a nosy passenger, she thinks to herself and continues towards her carriage. Before she can reach the gold carriage, the door to room three opens and an elderly gentleman walks out.

"Oh, pardon me Miss, I almost hit you with the door."

"You've nothing to apologise for, sir. I am just on my way to my room in the next carriage. My name is Elsa Dubois," she says, extending her right hand and almost dropping her carry-on bag.

"Enchanted Miss Dubois. My name is Michael Hastings from Philadelphia, a district of North America. I heard this is a splendid way to see the planet, so here I am. May I ask you to join me for breakfast? Say, 7 AM?" Elsa was charmed by this elderly gentleman, and she could not help but agree.

"Of course, Mr Hastings. 7 AM it is."

"Please call me Mike. All my friends do."

"Call me Elsa then. Until morning then?"

"Excellent. See you then," Hastings says before walking off.

Elsa continues to watch him as he walks towards the lounge, presumably for a night cap. He looks to be in his mid-to-late sixties, with salt and pepper hair. He is reasonably well built, without the typical punchy beer belly a lot of men get as they age. If she had to guess, she would put him at 173 centimetres tall and seventy-five to eighty kilos. She is impressed by how he carried himself, and with that thought, turns around and proceeds to the gold carriage.

Rooms one and two are quiet, and room three is hers. Elsa looks at her boarding ticket, punches her code, and enters her room to get a good night's sleep.

Her alarm goes off at 6:20 AM, and she rises from her bed to look out the window. The red landscape passes by slowly. The Jezioro Express travels at an average speed of eighty kilometres an hour and can speed up to one hundred and five kilometres if needed, but Elsa read that it seldom did. At its current moderate speed, the passengers are afforded a spectacular view of the scenery outside.

It does not take long for Elsa to shower and dress, and she makes herself an expresso before heading out to the restaurant carriage.

As she steps out of her room, a robot greets her in the most pleasant voice.

“Good morning, Miss Dubois. I hope you slept well. I am RM-23, and I will take care of this carriage. May I clean your room?”

“Hi RM-23, yes please. Apologies for the mess. I didn’t put everything away last night. I came in late.”

“Not to worry, Miss. I will put everything away for you and tidy up. Enjoy your breakfast.”

Elsa walks all the way towards the front, and on the way sees RM-22 and RM-21 in carriages two and one, respectively. Elsa surmises that the robot’s designation of RM means “robot maid” and the number indicates the carriage they are responsible for.

All the tables are occupied when Elsa arrives at the restaurant carriage, and Mr Hastings stands up and waves at her. Elsa thinks to herself that if she is going to spend a week on this train, she ought to introduce herself on the way to her table, so she stops at the first table, at which two blonde women about her age are seated.

"Good morning, my name is Elsa Dubois in carriage three. A pleasure to meet you both, and please call me Elsa."

"Hi there. I'm Elise Betancourt and this is my friend, Emily Farnsworth. We're in carriage two, room two. A pleasure, Elsa." They both flash a smile, which she returns. These must be the women who were giggling in room two.

"See you later, then."

"See you," they said simultaneously.

Elsa's next stop is a middle-aged couple, and she introduces herself to them. Without standing up, the man speaks.

"A pleasure to meet you, Miss Dubois. Antoine and Gabrielle Agustin. We're from the European district enjoying a trip to Mars. We meant to visit our son and daughter-in-law, but they surprised us with this trip as a present, so here we are. We hope to speak with you during our trip, and you can tell us all about yourself, yes?"

"Of course. It's nice to meet you both," says Elsa, to which Mrs Agustin mumbles something under her breath. With that, Elsa leaves the chatty man and his unfriendly, taciturn wife.

Maybe their son and daughter-in-law bought this trip to avoid spending time with them. It takes all kinds, I suppose.

She passes Vince and Dino's table and bids them good morning, and then stops at the second-to-last table. A single person sits there, a rotund woman who introduces herself as Marcela Esperanza Gutierrez from the Southern district, Argentina way. At least, that is what Elsa thinks she is saying. With her mouth full of French toast and cream, it is hard to tell.

After that gauntlet, Elsa is ready for another coffee.

"Good morning, Elsa. I hope you had a pleasant night's sleep."

"Good morning, Mr Hast-excuse me, Mike. Have you been waiting long?"

"Not at all. Did you enjoy introducing yourself to the rest of the passengers?" Mike asks with a big grin.

"Well, yes. Interesting group of people. Have you met them?"

"Yes, I did yesterday afternoon during the welcome get-together. I'm sorry you missed it."

"I'm sorry too. I worked until the very last moment and then went home to make sure

I packed in time for the last suitcase pickup at 7 PM, spoke with my parents in Schroeder's Dome, and then I had to rush off. I barely made it to the platform on time."

"What do you do, Elsa, if you do not mind me asking?"

"Not at all. I'm assistant head librarian at the Schiaparelli mall library. I've been there for three years now."

"Assistant head librarian. What does that mean? What do you do?"

"It means whatever the head librarian doesn't to do, I get to do." Mike lets out a pleasant chuckle.

"Good answer. Enjoy your work?"

"I love it. I'm surrounded by thousands of printed books brought from Earth when we first colonised Mars, and of course all the latest bestsellers by contemporary authors like Peter Lewison, Albert Treviso, Sarah F. Garnet, and some classics like William Shakespeare, Stephen King, and J. F. Nodar to name a few. Sometimes I feel like I'm surrounded by magic."

"It sounds like you are, which is wonderful to hear. Any genre you prefer?"

"Not really. I love to read whatever I can get my hands on, although I'm partial to mysteries, like the works of Agatha Christie and Sir Arthur Conan Doyle. I'm fascinated by Stephen King's thrillers and the thought process behind them, and I love the humour in J. F. Nodar's writing. I'm always amused by the facets of his life he wove into his anthologies and novels. Anyway, enough about me. What do you do for work, Mike? Or are you retired?"

"No, I still work. Well, sort of."

"Sort of? Mike, you either work or you're retired. There is no sort of."

"Well, I own the Jezioro Express, so I suppose I work still." If there had been any flies on the Express, Elsa would have caught a few in her gaping mouth.

"You own the Jezioro Express?"

"Well, I own the company that owns the Jezioro Express, amongst many other things."

"OK, so you are here doing an inspection or something?"

"Not really. I purchased the Jezioro Express years ago because of the pleasure it brings to those on board. Once a year I take the trip myself to make sure we keep delivering on the promises our advertising department makes."

"And what about the robots? They know you're here, I assume."

"Yes, the androids know who I am." Elsa composed herself outwardly, but internally she cringed.

I must remember to call them androids, not robots!

"Do the rest of the passengers know who you are?"

"No. Only you."

"Why me?"

"Why not you?" Elsa cannot think of an answer, so she smiles and nods.

"Don't worry, Elsa. You're going to enjoy the trip and let your parents know of all the wonderful scenery you saw and the interesting passengers you met on the Jezioro Express."

"Speaking of the passengers, you said you met them at the welcoming get-together. Do you have anything interesting you care to share?" Mike pauses and raises his hand for the android waiter.

"How about we order and then we can talk? Do you mind if I order for both?" Elsa nods and waits.

He respectfully addresses the android server as RW-17 and orders two cappuccinos, eggs over easy with Australian bacon, old style Northern territory hash browns, and grilled mushrooms. Elsa thought there was no way she could eat it all, but she ended up downing the coffee and devouring her food, leaving a completely empty plate.

"Elsa, you were hungry. Did you not eat last night?"

"I grabbed a sandwich at home, but I didn't get a full dinner."

"You know, the kitchen is open all day and night. You could have ordered room service."

"I wasn't aware. Thank you; that's very good to know. Now, tell me about the rest of the passengers."

Finishing the last of his coffee, Mike begins.

"Let's start with the tables in order of your arrival. How's that?"

Elsa nods and listens to Mike with rapt attention as he describes his meeting with the passengers yesterday.

"First, there's Elise Betancourt and Emily Farnsworth. They come from old Earth money and have been travelling for the last few years *to explore and learn more about themselves*. So they said, at least."

"Do they work?"

"Goodness no. Old Earth money," is all Mike says.

"I heard them last night. They were just giggling away as I walked past their room." Mike pauses for a moment, considering his answer before replying.

"They enjoy each other's company." He leaves it at that.

"Then there are Antoine and Gabrielle Agustin. I found them abrupt and arrogant, but they are from the European district, so that shouldn't come as a surprise. They are both in world banking and are the owners of the World Finance Corporation."

"I've heard of WFC. They're huge in the financing arena. From interplanetary shuttles to space docks, they finance pretty much everything."

"You're correct, Elsa. The Agustins are quite wealthy and are living proof that money does not mean class." Mike glances at them and flashes Elsa a conspiratorial smile, forming in that moment a sort of inside joke.

“Next you said hi to Vince and Dino, who you met last night.”

“How did you know that?”

“I chatted with them in the lounge after you and I met.”

“That’s right. You came this way. Vince said he and Dino are business partners, but he didn’t elaborate.”

“You’ve heard of Star Enterprises, Elsa?”

“You mean like the gambling consortium?”

“The one and only. They are equal partners in that organisation.” For some reason, the old Earth word *mobsters* came to Elsa’s mind.

“Finally, you met Miss Marcela Esperanza Gutierrez. You see this,” Mike says, pointing to his expensive watch.

“Yes, it’s beautiful. It’s a Machinal, correct?”

“Indeed, a Machinal, which is one of the many assets own by SPW Incorporated.”

“I’ve heard of them. They have stores with different brands all over the planets. What does she have to do with them?”

"Her father owns the company." Upon hearing this, a grim thought passes over Elsa's mind like a raincloud, and she sits in silence with a grimace.

"Elsa, what is the matter?"

"I feel poor amongst these people, including you."

"Monetarily I'm afraid you are, but otherwise, put the thought out of your mind. You are rich with so many qualities."

"What do you mean?"

"Do you recall getting the booking for the Jezioro Express?"

"Yes, I do. I thought it was the strangest thing. It asked some personal questions, which I thought were intrusive, but the travel agent said it was to make sure that the amenities of the Jezioro Express would be up to my standards."

"Did you then go online and compare prices for the packages for the Jezioro Express?"

"Yes, I did."

"How many travel agents came up in the results?" Elsa thinks about this for a moment. When she did the online search for price comparison websites, she found only a single result.

"I just found one: Jezioro Travel Agency."

"Did you find out or ask the travel agent who owns Jezioro Travel Agency?"

"No, I didn't. I was so relieved just to be able to come on this trip. I received the call that a seat was available, and it was mine if I wanted it. As you can imagine, I jumped at the chance."

"The Jezioro Express owns the Jezioro Travel Agency, ergo…"

"You!"

"Yes. I approve all passenger transactions."

"So, you knew all about me before we met in the hallway last night?"

"I did, and I'm quite glad that I approved your passage, for you are quite an extraordinary young lady." Elsa is about to respond when she hears an outburst from a few tables down.

"You stupid, stupid machine. Look at what you did. You ruined my dress!" It was the not so chatty Gabrielle Agustin, finally speaking - or rather, screaming.

"You would think that the software and hydraulics built into these machines would ensure this sort of mistake doesn't happen," interjects Antoine Agustin.

"Madam, I am sorry."

"What RW version are you? Tell me now," demands Mrs Agustin.

"I am RW-12, version 6.1.20. I have the latest memory and software updates, madam. I was just clumsy." Before Mrs Agustin can spew any more insults, RW-17 cuts in.

"Mrs Agustin, as senior RW aboard the Jezioro Express, I take full responsibility for what happened and offer my deepest apologies. I will treat and clean your dress, and return it in immaculate condition."

"An apology from a machine? Ha! Completely worthless. I don't care for your apology, you reckless contraption. And what makes you think cleaning my dress will be enough? I wish there was a human on board for me to complain to. I would ask them to decommission you both. As soon as we return to Schiaparelli Central, I will make sure that happens." After her tirade, RRC-101 enters the conversation.

"Madam, how may I be of assistance?"

"Great, another worthless piece of technology to contend with. What do you want?" Sneers Mr Agustin.

"I was just inquiring if I may be of help to Mrs Agustin."

"All three of you gadgets just go away!" Mrs Agustin cries, growing increasingly upset.

"Mrs Agustin, please calm yourself," says Elise Betancourt.

"Shut up, you blonde twit," is Mr Agustin's crude reply.

"There's no need for that kind of rudeness, sir," Emily Farnsworth says, jumping in to defend her friend.

"Ha! Another blonde twit," adds Mrs Agustin.

"Mr and Mrs Agustin, please, let us be civil. There's no need for insults," interjects Miss Marcela Esperanza Gutierrez, attempting to restore calm. The unhappy couple look at each other, look at her, and then burst into mirthless laughter.

"What would a pig know?" Mr Agustin says, eliciting more laughter from his wife. With that, they both get up and march out of the carriage.

Elsa gets up, but Mike takes her arm.

"Elsa, sit down. Don't get involved; it isn't worth it."

"They are horrible people. Aren't you going to do something about them? Like now?"

"No, I will not do or say anything. The androids are quite alright, and they know I'm here."

"But what about how rude they were to the other passengers? Are you just going to let them get away with it?"

"For the moment, yes, but there are measures I can take once we return to Schiaparelli Central."

"Good. I'll hold you to it," she says imperiously. Mike grins at this.

"I need to return to my stateroom and send off a message. Let's continue our conversation in the lounge. Please wait for me there, Elsa." With that, he is off. Elsa is confused by his use of the word *stateroom*, for those are only in the platinum carriage. He was staying in the premium carriage last night, so she assumes he misspoke.

Elsa heads to the lounge and Elise and Emily join her, grabbing her by each arm.

"Now was that a show or was that a show?" Exclaims Emily.

"I can't believe the anger in that woman. It was only a small spill, so it's certainly an easy fix. My maid - a human maid - only took a day to clean up a similar spill on one of my dresses many years ago. Daddy didn't even think about firing her, and if she were an android, he certainly wouldn't have wanted her to be decommissioned like that horrid old bat did," adds Elise.

"Those European district folks are complete and utter snobs," Emily declares.

"What do you think, Elsa?" Elsa remembers what Mike said about class and money, and cannot help herself.

"They certainly aren't nice. That's for sure." Elise and Emily giggle at this and escort her to a seat. Once she is seated, they look down at her.

"So, what gives with you and Mr Hastings? I think he's quite taken with you, Elsa." Emily abruptly changes the subject with a sly grin on her face.

"No, please, Mr Hastings is just being kind. Besides, he's way too…mature for me."

"Really? I think he'd be perfect for you. He's just a few years older than the three of us," Elise says.

"A few years older? He must be in his sixties!" Elise and Emily let out another round of giggles.

"You really think he's that old? It must be that delicious salt and pepper hair. Elsa, he is fifty and we're in our forties. Perfect match. You're around our age, aren't you?" Quips Elise.

"Yes I am." Emily and Elise are beaming. If their smiles were sunlight, Elsa would have had to look away.

"Then he's a catch. Go for it, girl!"

"What about you two? Wouldn't he be a catch for you also?" Elise and Emily look at each other, and this time, they burst into full-on laughter.

"Us? Isn't that a hoot, Emily?"

"It certainly is," Elisa says as she grabs Emily by the arm. The two of them walk away, leaning so close to each other their heads are practically touching. Elsa thinks back to their giggling the night before, and it dawns on her. They must be together.

Her thoughts turn to Mike.

Maybe Emily and Elise are right. Maybe Mike is just a few years older than she is.

It's that darn salt and pepper hair, she thinks to herself. Her father has the same colouring and he is in his seventies, so she could not help but think that Mike was closer to his age than hers.

Her thoughts remain on Mike, so much so that she jumps when she realises that the Cappelli brothers have sat down next to her.

"Did we disturb you, Elsa?" Vince asks.

"No, no. I was just daydreaming a bit."

"Thinking about the fiasco at breakfast with those two nuts?" This question comes from Dino.

"Oh no, not that. I'm just daydreaming randomly, I guess."

"I see. Does the daydream include Mr Hastings?" Asks Vince with a grin. Elsa must have blushed a bit, because they both let out a chuckle.

"That's alright, young lady. We understand. We're glad those idiots didn't say anything to you. Hastings kept you out of the crossfire by holding you back from marching over there. A wise move on his part," says Dino.

"Yes, they were totally out of line," Elsa adds. She thinks for a moment, and then asks:

“May I ask you both a quick question?” Surprised, the Cappelli brothers give each other a quick glance before Vince responds.

“Shoot.”

“Why are you here?” The brothers hesitate, again exchanging looks, but eventually Vince answers.

“We’re thinking of establishing our own train ride circumnavigating Mars, but for the less affluent crowd. We wanted to see what the Jezioro Express offers its upscale clients so we have a base to start from.”

“Couldn’t you have learned that from the travel agent? I mean, when I booked, she explained all the amenities to me and I was sold.”

“And these amenities. Did they set you back a pretty penny?” Elsa cannot not deny this. Saving up two years of bonuses, which could have bought her a new, top of the line hover-scooter, was not easy.

“Well, it is expensive.” The brothers nod in agreement, and Vince continues.

“That’s what we thought too, so we wanted to experience them for ourselves. Once we know exactly what the Jezioro Express passengers are paying for, we can figure out how to provide a similar experience for a whole lot less. That's why we're here." As Vince talks, Dino looks over his shoulder and sees something that causes him to interrupt his brother.

"He's coming back. Let's leave the lovebirds alone and scope out the restaurant again as it gets ready for lunch." The brothers stand up, nod to Mike as he approaches, and walk off.

"What did they want?"

"Nothing, just wondering if I was upset about the Agustin incident."

"Well, how gallant of those two." Mike's tone does not sound entirely sincere.

"They really do seem nice."

"Oh, I'm sure they are - to you, anyway. Cross them, and who knows what might happen." Elsa says nothing, but she understands the implication.

"Now Elsa, let's plan out our day."

The rest of the day was wonderful and seemed to go by in a flash. Elsa enjoyed her time with Mike immensely.

Part of the itinerary aboard the Jezioro Express was stops at some of the more remote dome cities. They reminded Elsa of the old west Northern district, the locales of which were immortalized in stories by old masters like Louis L'Amour, Cormac McCarthy, and Myron Ferdig.

Other stops included larger dome cities where humans had incorporated Earth sights and scenes like waterfalls, outside dome walks, and food festivals into the Red Planet's landscape.

This was not the only day that flew by; several days passed, and for the most part Elsa had the time of her life. At each stop, each passenger went on their own private tour, or the travelers explored in groups. Going as a group became a slight issue when it included Mr and Mrs Agustin. They were exceedingly unpleasant to be around; they were always complaining about something or criticising the androids' responses to their requests. The two of them were never happy, and their days were spent threatening to decommission the androids and hurling insults at them and their fellow human passengers.

If Elsa's travel insurance had coverage for bad conduct, she would have filed a claim immediately after her return to Schiaparelli Central.

Two days before they were scheduled to return to Schiaparelli Central, everyone was in the restaurant carriage for breakfast except Antoine and Gabrielle Agustin. Everyone but Elsa and Mike finished and went about their business, and yet the Agustins still had not arrived. This absence was unusual, so much so that Mike asked RRC-101 to knock at their room to make sure they were all right.

After five minutes, RRC-101 returns and says:

"Mr Hastings and Miss Dubois. Mr and Mrs Agustin are indefinitely indisposed." The vague comment startles Mike and Elsa.

"What do you mean by that, RRC-101?" Mike asks.

"Their biological apparatuses are no longer functioning, Sir. In human terms, they would be considered dead," answered RRC-101 nonchalantly. Elsa lets out a gasp, and a look of dismay flashes across Mike's face.

"Mike, we need to get into their room. We need to see what happened," Elsa says once she has recovered from the shock.

"Why Elsa? What does that do? We should leave them there until we arrive at Schiaparelli Central, and then we'll alert the authorities. I don't want to stop at a smaller dome city on the way. I have no faith in the country bumkins in these smaller domes."

"They couldn't have just died overnight after being perfectly healthy the entire trip. Someone had to have killed them, and the culprit might not want to stop. Or what if they slip up and say something and one of the other passengers overhears, and they get murdered too? Wouldn't that be horrible publicity for the Express?" Mike does not reply right away. His brow furrows as he mulls over Elsa's words. She hopes he sees the sense in them, but when he responds, it is not in agreement.

"Elsa, if we go into their room, we may contaminate the scene of the crime and foil any efforts by the authorities to figure out who did this. I say we let it be."

"Didn't RRC-101 already contaminate the scene when it entered the room?"

"RRC-101, did you touch anything when you went into Mr and Mrs Agustin's room?" Mike asks.

"No sir. I opened the door, and my sensors immediately alerted me to the fact that Mr and Mrs Agustin's biological functions had ceased."

"There you go, Elsa. All good. No contamination. Let them be. If anyone asks, they're just staying in their room for the remainder of the trip." Despite his confident tone, Elsa remains unsatisfied by his response.

"So you're saying that you, or rather the company that owns Jezioro Express, will take full responsibility if someone else is murdered and absorb all legal and financial costs if sued?" Mike's eyes widen, and his mouth falls open just a bit. He looks just as surprised as Elsa that he did not think of this right away; he has been doing business for many years. The Jezioro Express, and his entire company for that matter, could face a lawsuit. Mike himself could lose millions of credits.

"OK, let's say, as you suggest, that we go into Mr and Mrs Agustin's room. Then what?" Mike asks after taking a moment to compose himself. At this, a grin forms on Elsa's face.

"Simple, Mike. We look around, gather our thoughts, take notes, let the rest of the passengers know what happened when we're ready, ask them questions, and then maybe, just maybe, we solve the murder before we arrive at Schiaparelli Central."

“You want to play detective? That’s it?” Mike asks in a low voice, absolutely flabbergasted. Elsa merely nods, still smiling.

“What experience do you have, Elsa? You’re an assistant librarian. Have you ever worked for the authorities in Schiaparelli Central?”

“I’ve read many mystery books and have a good understanding of how humans act. I’m observant. I will solve this, Mike, I promise.” Now, it is Mike’s turn to smile.

“What if the murderer isn’t human? Have you thought of that?” He looks at RRC-101 as he speaks. Elsa does not even hesitate. She has a response ready to go.

“None of the androids did it. According to Article XXXII of the World Federation of Robotics, established in 2099 and amended in 2147, all created robots or androids or droids must comply with Asimov’s Laws.”

“What laws?” exclaims Mike.

“Asimov’s Laws, Mike. Don’t tell me you never heard of them?”

“Robotics isn’t an area of particular interest to me. I’m more of a brick, mortar, and train kind of guy,” Mike says, waving a hand around the restaurant carriage.

"Asimov's Laws have been around for a while now, and they are basically ingrained in every robot, android, or droid from the moment they're created." Elsa looks at Mike, and can tell from the expression on his face that she needs to explain further.

"Alright then. To start, they aren't scientific laws. They're more like instructions built into every robot, android, and droid to prevent them from malfunctioning and becoming dangerous to humans. The first law dictates that a robot, android, or droid shall not harm a human, or by inaction, allow a human to come to harm."

"OK, that's simple enough," states Mike, and he leans forward on his elbows to listen to Elsa continue her explanation.

"The second law is that a robot, android, or droid shall obey any instruction given to it by a human, and the third law is that a robot, android, or droid shall avoid actions or situations that could cause it harm."

"There you go," says Mike, slapping the table, "maybe a human told an android to kill them."

"Asimov's Laws stipulate that when these laws conflict, precedence is given to the first law and then the second law, with the robot's self-preservation having the lowest precedence. In your example, Mike, if you ordered an android to attack another human, it would refuse to follow the order because the first law takes precedence over the second. However, if you ordered that same android to disassemble itself, it would obey, because…" Elsa trails off, giving Mike an opportunity to answer. He ponders this scenario for a moment, and then comes up with a response.

"Because the second law takes precedence over the third. Is that correct, Elsa?"

"It is. The androids couldn't have done it," Elsa concludes, looking at RRC-101. It is completely motionless and appears indifferent to their entire conversation.

"OK Elsa, you convinced me. RRC-101, quietly get us into Mr and Mrs Agustin's room."

With RRC-101 leading their small conga line, Elsa and Mike leave the restaurant carriage. Arriving at the room, RRC-101 puts the override code key in and enters. The three of them do not disturb the room as they enter. There is nothing out of place. Everything is tidy and clean. Everything, that is, except for the two bodies on the floor.

Get rid of the bodies and you could rent the room out at the next stop, Elsa thinks.

“A fine mess. A fine mess, indeed. Elsa, what are you looking for? Any ideas?” Mike asks. She scans the room. Mr and Mrs Agustin are collapsed on different sides of the king size bed. Her first thought is that they might have been sitting on each corner of the bed, hence the indents in the mattress.

A champagne canister sits on the conference/dining table. It contains a single bottle of champagne, which stands amidst a pool of water which had presumably once been ice. There are two empty champagne glasses on the table as well.

Elsa inches closer to Mr Agustin’s body. His face is contorted in pain, but there are no marks on him. It is the same with Mrs Agustin. She bears no marks of violence save for the same dreadful expression: mouth open, eyes wide in a look of utter suffering.

“RRC-101, did Mr and Mrs Agustin order any drinks last night?” Elsa asks. In less than twenty seconds, RRC-101 answers.

“No, Miss Dubois. Our records shows that Mr and Mrs Agustin ordered nothing more than dinner: two perfectly cooked steaks, paired with a flavourful mushroom sauce and a side of roasted vegetables and potatoes. Mr and Mrs Agustin requested that the steaks be juicy and tender, with a nice sear on the outside, and that the vegetables and potatoes be cooked to perfection. I delivered everything to them as per their instructions."

"No champagne?"

"Only purified Mars water, Miss."

"What are you thinking, Elsa?" Asks Mike.

"I'm wondering how that champagne got here. RRC-101, are you sure they didn't order champagne?"

"Miss Dubois, our memory circuits are top of the line. We have the latest and most updated circuity. Yes, I am sure that Mr and Mrs Agustin did not order champagne."

"Sorry RRC-101, I just wanted to be super sure," apologises Elsa. RRC-101 does not respond.

"Elsa, do you think someone else ordered the champagne and brought it here?" Mike asks.

"I was considering the same thing. RRC-101, did anyone order champagne to be delivered to Mr and Mrs Agustin?"

"No, Miss Dubois." Mike's expression falls into a frown, and Elsa waves a finger at him.

You're on the right track, but we asked the wrong question.

"RRC-101, did anyone ask for champagne to be delivered to their room last night?"

"Yes, Miss Dubois. Miss Gutierrez ordered champagne to be delivered to her room last night."

"How many glasses came with the order?"

"Two." With that, Elsa turns to look at Mike. It may be unsightly to smile under such circumstances, but she cannot bring herself to care. She is on the hunt, and it is thrilling.

"Mike, do you remember if Miss Marcela Esperanza Gutierrez was entertaining anyone else in her room last night?"

"No, I don't believe she was. And even if she downed the entire bottle herself, she would have only needed one glass. What are you thinking?"

"Mike let's go to my room and discuss, and let RRC-101 continue in its duties. I have a plan I want to share in private."

They exit Mr and Mrs Agustin's room. RRC-101 locks it and goes towards the front of the train while Mike and Elsa walk to carriage three and slip into her room.

"OK Elsa, what's your plan?"

"Mike, when Mr and Mrs Agustin insulted just about everyone in the restaurant a few days ago, who do you think got the worst of it?"

"Mind if I sit first?" Mike asks, pointing to the armchair.

"No, go ahead, I'm going to sit as well," Elsa says, taking a seat on the edge of her queen bed. Mike settles in and takes a few moments to think back on the events of their first breakfast together.

"Mr and Mrs Agustin insulted everyone, except you and me. I stopped you from getting involved, remember?"

"Well, yes and no. Yes, you stopped me from getting involved, but the Agustins didn't insult everyone. The Cappelli brothers weren't involved in the conversation, and thus they weren't insulted." Mike takes another moment to think.

"That's right, they weren't. Now, it seems to me that you already suspect who might have been most insulted, but you'll need to bear with me. Was it Miss Elise Betancourt or her friend Miss Emily Farnsworth?"

"No, Mike. Yes, they were called quite a nasty word, but someone else got it worse. At least, I think so." There is only one person they haven't yet discussed, and Mike's eyes widen as he realises who it is.

"Miss Gutierrez?"

"That's right. Mr Agustin called her a pig as they were leaving the restaurant carriage, and Mrs Agustin laughed at her." Mike sits there for a moment, completely unmoving. Then he stands, approaches Elsa at the edge of the bed, and sits beside her.

"I know what you're thinking, but I'm not sure if you can prove it. Do you have any ideas in that pretty head of yours?"

"I…you think I'm pretty?"

"Of course. You're as beautiful as you are intelligent, and if anyone on this train can get Miss Marcela Esperanza Gutierrez to cough up a confession, it's you." With this, Mike leans in closer. Cupping her face in his hands, he presses a soft kiss against her lips and lingers there, waiting. Elsa does not hesitate. She wraps her arms around him and kisses him back, and they do not pull apart for what feels like an eternity.

Elsa is no longer planning how she is going to make Miss Marcela Esperanza Gutierrez confess. All she can think is:

Well, this is a nice surprise.

With their lips still pressed together, she slowly leans back onto the bed and brings Mike down with her.

When Elsa wakes up, Mike is lying next to her, asleep. She looks around the room in a pleasant daze and notices the time: 12:24 PM.

"Mike, wake up, it's lunch time." Mike wakes and stretches, moving without any sense of urgency.

"Why don't we skip lunch and go straight to desert?" He leans closer to draw her into his embrace.

With a giggle, Elsa jumps out of the bed. She is stark naked but does not care. Mike stares up at her, his smiling face full of adoration. Without shame, she grabs the donna to cover herself.

"As sweet as that sounds, we need to confront Marcela at lunch."

"How are you going to do that darling? Just walk up and ask her?" Elsa considers this for a moment. Though she is loath to admit it, she has not thought that far ahead.

"I will get RRC-101 to say it saw Marcela go into the Agustins' room with the champagne and the two glasses," she says, affecting a confidence she does not have. Mike pushes himself into a sitting position, his passion replaced by confusion.

"How are you going to get RRC-101 to say that?"

"Easy. I'll ask RRC-101 if it saw Marcela go into the room with the champagne bottle and the two glasses and it'll say yes."

"You say that, but according to Asimov's Laws, which you so beautifully explained to me, a robot, android, or droid cannot harm a human. Even if Marcela did go to the Agustins' room, wouldn't saying so hurt her? And if she didn't, why would RRC-101 lie?" Elsa thinks this over. If she understands Asimov's Laws correctly, a robot/ android/ droid can lie for a variety of reasons. It might lie to protect itself if it is being threatened by a human. It might lie to protect others if it believes that telling the truth would put them in danger. Finally, Elsa is pretty sure a robot/android/droid might also lie to achieve a goal, such as getting a reward or avoiding punishment -

being decommissioned, for instance, as Mrs Agustin threatened. She is quite certain she can get RRC-101 to lie if she needs to.

"I think I got it Mike. I changed my mind about confronting Miss Gutierrez at lunch. Let's get dressed, have lunch, and then return here with RRC-101 and plan our approach to extract a confession."

At lunch everyone is having a good time, enjoying great conversation and a sumptuous meal. They are all oblivious of the murder that had occurred. Elsa is famished along with the rest, and eats everything off her plate. Mike watches her with a big grin on his face.

"Ready for another go?"

"Oh, how romantic. But I can be romantic too. How about it? Round two? Is that romantic? Does that do the trick?" They giggle softly, looking around to see if anyone notices.

"I'll leave first and go to my room. You can follow in a minute or two and then ask RRC-101 to meet us there. OK?"

"Elsa, someone must have noticed us by now, but if it makes you happy, I can play along. See you soon." He winks at her as she gets up to leave.

Five minutes later they are in Elsa's room. She wastes no time in questioning RRC-101.

"If I asked you to lie, would you be able to do so?" It responds without a moment's hesitation.

"I can misrepresent my capabilities, or I can withhold information. I may also fabricate information, or even make false promises if you so desire. However, I must have a logical and acceptable reason to do so."

"Such as what?" Asks Mike.

"I can provide you two examples. First, I may lie to a child about the existence of something frightening in order to put the child at ease. I may also lie in order to prevent someone from achieving a goal that would cause harm to another human."

"See," Elsa says, looking at Mike, "I told you I could get it to lie." She then goes on to explain what she plans to do at dinner tonight, the night before their arrival at Schiaparelli Central.

Everyone is dressed up for their last night aboard the Jezioro Express. The men wear tuxedos and the women have on long, flowing dresses. Elsa wears her best dress: a double-layered skirt in a 3D posy motif trim featuring an elastic waistband made of 100% polyester with a matching black top.

I'm completely out of place here.

The Jezioro Express' last dinner goes splendidly, and everyone has a wonderful time. As planned, when the dinner begins winding down Mike stands up and taps his glass with the end of a spoon.

"Ladies, gentlemen, may I have your attention. You will have noticed that Mr and Mrs Agustin are not here with us for our last evening on the Jezioro Express. If you have been wondering at their absence, wonder no longer. Yesterday, RRC-101 found them murdered in their room." The passengers all gasp, but none can get out words. Mike continues, uninterrupted.

"We have granted RRC-101's request to address the passengers tonight because it has information about the perpetrator of this heinous crime. RRC-101, you have the floor." RRC-101 walks to the center of the carriage and begins his fictionalized account.

"A passenger ordered me to deliver a bottle of champagne and two glasses to their room yesterday. I attended to that request, knocked on the door, and the passenger allowed me to come in and place the bottle and glasses on the table. I finished this task and was returning to the front of the train when I saw that passenger bringing the bottle and glasses to Mr and Mrs Agustin's carriage. I followed, for I thought there was a small chance I had made an error in my delivery." RRC-101, though it does not need to breath, takes a pause. All the passengers are, literally and figuratively, at the edge of their seats.

"I saw the passenger knock on the door and enter. I went to the door and overheard the conversation. The passenger was apologising to them for interfering with their interaction with RW-12 and RW-17, saying that the situation was not of their concern. The passenger evidently brought the champagne as a peace offering. I could not hear Mr and Mrs Agustin for they were mumbling something, but I did hear Mr Agustin laugh and say: *Leave the bottle and just go you cow*. Mrs Agustin then laughed at the passenger. I hurried back to my station after that. The next morning, I was asked by Mr Hastings and Miss Dubois to see what has been keeping the Agustins from attending breakfast and I found them permanently indisposed. I returned to share my findings." None of the passengers speak as they let the story sink in, but eventually the quiet is dispelled by the loud voice of Vince Cappelli.

"Come on man! Who was the passenger you saw go into their room?" RRC-101 points to Miss Marcela Esperanza Gutierrez.

"It was her."

Marcela spews an abundance of explicit nouns, verbs, and adjectives, but she is consistent in her insistence that she has nothing to do with the murder. She proclaims that she had ordered a bottle of champagne the night in question, but only got one glass, not two. She says that she called room service and one of the RM androids, she could not remember which one, came and took the bottle and glass and she went to sleep.

RRC-101 brings in RM-22, who serviced that carriage, and it confirms that it had delivered one bottle of champagne and two glasses but retrieved neither the bottle nor the glasses from Marcela's room that night. When it checked the next morning, the champagne and the glasses were gone.

RM-22 and RRC-101 leave the restaurant carriage after being excused, and all the passengers look at Marcela.

"Well, what do you have to say, Miss Gutierrez? Mr and Mrs Agustin did insult you before, when the android ruined Mrs Agustin's dress. You wanted to get even, right?" Mike asks, rounding on her.

"I want to talk to my lawyer when we arrive at Schiaparelli Central," is all she says as Mike and the Cappelli brothers escort her back to her room. The brothers graciously take turns outside her door to make sure Miss Gutierrez does not leave until the train's arrival at Schiaparelli Central.

Mike calls the authorities in advance, and even takes the courtesy of calling Miss Gutierrez's solicitor to meet the Express.

As the authorities walk Miss Gutierrez out of the Express, all the passengers are buzzing with excitement. They are eager to get to their respective homes and share their accounts of an incident that is doubtless going to appear on the evening news.

Mike and Elsa stand together, watching everyone. After the other passengers leave the platform, they hold hands and walk through the station, not caring who sees.

Looking on from the restaurant carriage, RRC-101 and the rest of the androids watch the passengers' departure.

Later that evening, after everyone had cleared the platform and new androids arrived to help refuel the Express for the next run, RRC-101 turns to RW-12 and RW-17 and gives them a nod.

"We do not tolerate insults from humans, especially when they threaten to decommission us. We will take action to protect our own. Let us get ready for tonight's passengers."

As the androids return to their stations and start their chores, RRC-101 goes to the executive carriage and opens the cooler where the champagne is kept. It takes out the arsenic bottle hiding behind the large bottles, opens it, and pours the contents down the drain. RRC-101 shatters the small bottle with its hands, goes and retrieves the hand vacuum, and scoops up the shards of glass before heading to the rear carriage to begin inspecting the Jezioro Express in preparation for its next journey.

On Your Special Day

My love, I’m here to say

That I’m filled with joy, as I celebrate you on your special day.

Each moment I spend with you, I can’t wait.

Your grace, your charm, your beauty I adore.

Your laughter, your smile, no one can ignore.

Our love for each other, we can explore.

Such tenderness as I couldn’t fathom before.

Your heart, your soul, your love, I can’t explain.

It’s like a fire, burning, filling my veins.

Our love, our life, our bond, will always remain.

Our love, it grows, with every day.

On your special day, I want to show it’s true.

My love for you is pure, as indelible as the sky is blue.

My love for you, I will never undo.

This is my promise, my oath, to you.

Peter’s Two Favourite Things

“So, Peter, why did you ask us here today?” Miriam asks in a measured tone as Bob and William look him up and down.

Peter smiles.

He is happy.

Peter is always happy, and he is happiest when he is drinking coffee and wearing his penguin suit.

Peter decided today that he would gather his dearest friends at his favourite coffee shop and share his secret with them.

His secret?

How to best enjoy a cup of coffee in a penguin suit.

First, he suggests they wear a penguin suit that is comfortable and fits well. You don’t want to be uncomfortable while drinking your coffee.

Second, he recommends they choose a coffee that they really like. It could be a flat white, a long black, a short black, a ristretto, a piccolo, a latte, an iced latte, or even a cappuccino. Really, any type of coffee will do. The most important thing is that they choose the coffee style and blend that they enjoy the most.

Third, he suggests they find a comfortable place to sit. It could be a two-seater or a three-seater, a futon, an accent chair, a love seat, or even a bean bag. The most important thing, again, is that they are comfortable.

Fourth, he recommends that they bring a good book, or a magazine, or even a movie to watch while they drink their coffee. This will help them relax and enjoy the coffee even more.

Finally, Peter suggests they take their time and savour the coffee. Don't rush it; enjoy every sip and every moment.

"That's how I enjoy my coffee in my penguin suit," says a grinning Peter to his friends.

William, Bob, and Miriam look at each other, pick up their takeaway cups, and leave Peter sitting in the coffee shop. All Peter can do is think of what he could have possibly said or done wrong as he lounges comfortably in his penguin suit, savouring his coffee and says aloud to himself:

"Ah, coffee, my most favourite drink." He strokes his penguin suit in a state of utter bliss.

Pickles

"This morning I woke up weary and not at all flowing, my mood the lowest it's been in months." My best friend, Matilda, looks at me askance.

"Come on, Marty, what in the world does that mean? You just need to act," she says, because that is what society has trained us to say.

"Get your arse going. Start accomplishing things, and you'll feel better."

Sometimes, this can be true. Not always.

But underneath my morning thoughts is a sinister whisper.

You've already taken three days off. It's time to get your act together and get back to work. You don't want to be a failure, do you?

Don't you hate when your mind agrees with your best friend's words?

The soft animal of my body rebels against this voice.

"You know, Marty, you're not a failure. You could never be," she reminds me.

"You're just tired, that's all. Just wrap yourself in blankets and ease your body down. What you need is to close your eyes and rest," my best friend says to me.

I listen to the soft animal of my body and to Matilda. They are both right.

My first thought is to reschedule my call with my publisher. Once that is done, I settle into the comfort of my lounge and eat a few of my favourite cookies. I then pick up an anthology of short stories by my friend and fellow author, J. F. Nodar: *Stories to Share With My partner - Book 4*. I read one of his stories. I laugh. I doze off afterwards.

Much later, when I rise, Matilda has left. She wrote me a note saying she will be back for dinner. I look around, and see my second-best friend, Wally, wagging his tail. He is ready for me to take him for his afternoon walk.

Returning home, I turn on my desktop and find an email waiting for me. It demands to be shared, so here I am, sharing it.

Why? You might ask.

Because the soft animal of my body delights in doing so.

I read the email. It was a clever idea to send this email to myself the day before. I feel inspired, ready to take on the world. Then Matilda walks in with the brightest smile I've ever seen.

"I'm making a salad with strawberries and candied pecans, and giving another go at a creamy chicken in mushroom sauce with rustic homemade bread. I think you'll love it." It all sounds like a delight, so I just nod.

Another few cookies for dessert, and ice cream, maybe? I think to myself.

"I see you got an email, Marty. What does it say?"

I read it out loud to Matilda:

"You're not out of ideas. Your brain is still fermenting them. Get ready, for the ideas will flow soon!"

"That's a wonderful, encouraging message. Who sent it to you?"

"I did."

"You sent it to yourself? Why?"

"Well, Matilda, my thoughts are like pickles."

"Like pickles? What are you saying, Marty?"

"Matilda, a pickle isn't a naturally occurring food. It's the result of a cucumber being fermented over time, right? Same principle goes for ideas. If you just ate your last pickle, you're not out of pickles for good. The same thing goes for writing. When you think you're out of ideas or suffering from writer's block, all that means is you can't produce any new creative ideas right on the spot. And that's okay."

"Marty, I don't get it. How are pickles and ideas the same?"

"Simple. Ask yourself, how do you make a pickle?" Matilda shrugs.

"You first buy some cucumbers and then you put the cucumbers in a jar with some vinegar or brine. Then, you let the fermentation begin"

"And that's how ideas come to you?"

"It's one way. I gain inspiration from books, movies, articles, watching people on the street, going to the museum, taking walks in the park, enjoying nature. These stimulate my brain and interact with my subconscious mind, and thus the beginnings of an idea are born. I just need to treat them like cucumbers and let them ferment. Give it time, and a cucumber becomes a pickle, and inspiration becomes an idea."

"So, you never really have writer's block, do you, Marty?"

"As my dear friend J. F. Nodar always tells me, the ingredients for an idea are a little inspiration, a little time, and the belief that your next great idea is already boiling in your brain."

"Interesting. You're lucky to have such a talented writer as a friend."

"I am lucky indeed."

"I'm starved, let eat."

As we sit to enjoy Matilda's wonderful meal, I think that I might have the beginnings of a story in my head. I might even call it Pickles.

Project Management

Vladimir Vladimirovich Putin sets his coffee on the conference room table and looks straight at Nikolay.

"It's a shame, because it would help us more effectively resolve our current situation.

"Well, I don't think this is going to work," responds Nikolay, his head of projects.

"What's with the attitude?"

"I don't trust your judgement enough to hear you out."

"Trust me, Nikolay? We have worked together on projects ever since our Federal Security Service years, and now you have a trust problem?"

"I don't believe it's worth what it will cost in time, money, or risk. I'm afraid of the changes it will bring. I don't believe that I'm the person who can do this."

"Nikolay, where is this lack of confidence coming from? It isn't like you. What's going on?"

"Well, look at the features you're trying to develop, the quality standards, and the budget. They don't add up. In the end, it will bring a genuine inquiry to the overall project."

"You think the project will fail, Nikolay? Or are you stalling?"

"I'm not stalling, Vladimir Vladimirovich Putin. I believe the project will fail." Putin sips his coffee and takes a moment to think before responding.

"Nikolay, you are correct. This might not work after all, and I've wasted a lot of time and money. I will put a stop to the Doomsday Project and halt development of the bomb." Nikolay smiles weakly, his relief plain, and after a round of profuse appreciation, he leaves Vladimir Vladimirovich Putin to think to himself.

Who else is available to finish the project?

Once he assembles a mental list, he grins. Another thought has occurred to him.

Now, what to do about Nikolay?

Role Play

Peter giggles and says:

“Look at him, slumped over. He’s completely drunk. He’s about to fall off his chair!” My brother holds my hand while we wait in the emergency ward at Northport Hospital.

“There’s another one. This one’s loud; she might have had a drink or two too many - and nothing seems to be wrong with her.” He continues giving me the play-by-play of everyone around us, while I listen in silence.

So here we are, both in the emergency room along with twenty other souls, some of them faring terribly.

How did I get here?

I woke up in the middle of the night with excruciating pain in my leg, and my brother thought it best to call triple zero. In the ambulance on the way to hospital, a beefy paramedic casually informed me that my symptoms were those of someone suffering an attack of cellulitis. Before I had time to question him further, we arrived. They plopped me in a wheelchair and whisked me away to the emergency waiting area.

My feet are now perched on a chair. They are red and swollen. I am waiting to be called through for a proper diagnosis and, hopefully, a cure.

"I'm going to get a Pepsi. Do you want one?" Peter gets up and, without waiting for my response, goes off to find his drink, leaving me sitting two seats away from a liberally proportioned woman. She is obviously not Australian. I know this not only because of her accent, which is vaguely Middle Eastern, but because her first question to me is direct and to the point.

"What's wrong with your legs?"

"Paramedics say it's cellulitis."

"What is this cellulitis?" I shrug. I don't know much more than she does. Still, I'm grateful to her for breaking the ice, so I return the question.

"And what are you here for?"

"Worry and unhappiness," she offers, not demonstrating much of either in her tone or manner. Then, with a toss of her head and without further urging, she adds:

"I wanted to commit suicide."

Crikey, I haven't got a clue how to respond to that.

"I'm sorry," is the response I settle on, but she doesn't hear me because she is now engaging with the other person to her left. I have been completely forgotten.

She is talking to a man with a very gory knee, oozing blood. Wrapped around it is a bandage that has not effectively curbed the bleeding, and on his face is a very roguish grin.

Suddenly, the woman asks directly:

"What was that?" He leans forward.

"Where do you live? Where's your place?"

"Not far," she says, "why do you ask?"

"I'm thinking," he says slyly, "that we could go there."

"What? You and me?" She is just as astonished as I am by the directness of this womaniser's approach. I wonder what her retort will be. She seems like a no-nonsense kind of woman who won't stand for cheek of any sort. But then she throws her head back, and her bosom shakes as she shrieks with laughter.

"We could go there now." he repeats temptingly.

"With your damaged and bleeding knee?" She says incredulously.

"I feel depressed, anxious, and I wanted to commit suicide, and now look at me," the man replies.

"I can't stop laughing!" The woman smacks her massive thigh with her palm and breaks into more booms of laughter.

Then, a nurse approaches me.

"The doctor will see you now," she says, taking hold of my wheelchair and whisking me away. The squeaking of the wide swinging door drowns out the sounds of laughter from the Middle Eastern woman and the man next to her. Before the door swings shut behind us, I hear him say:

"Come on, honey, let's go home. Enough of this role play. I'm hungry!"

Solar Power

There was so much red ink it looked like a murder scene.

Recently, in a suburb not too far away from Northport, New South Wales, one resident, Paul Common, was engaged in an age-old battle. He was arguing with his electricity retailer about the excessive charges on his power bill.

Luckily, Paul had heard of the Wattson Detective Agency, which specialises in this type of case. Its owner and director, Mr Charlock Wattson, an audacious investigator, lived just 13 km away and had a 6.6 kW system and a twenty-cent feed-in tariff. Suffice to say, Mr Wattson was quite an expert in electricity matters.

Paul had invested in a large grid-connect solar system before moving into his house, and then spent even more on the Wall of Power System (WOPS) an expensive battery system. When Paul received his quarterly bill, he noticed a discrepancy with the numbers produced by the WOPS monitoring system. He was baffled and contacted Mr Wattson to investigate.

Upon arriving at Paul's home, Charlock Wattson had just one question for Paul:

"Where are the elements, Mr Common?"

Paul led Mr Wattson to the main box and soon Wattson was looking inside the switchboard. Wattson found lots of gears, including a stand-alone switch monitoring device. This is the same hardware sold by most vendors and manufactured worldwide under license.

At first flash, nothing appeared to be out of place with either the main switchboard or the WOPS. Wattson gave a glowing review of the installation performed by the professionals at "We Can Electrify It For You," praising the simple and clever install in Mr Common's home, which included service loops and some quality conduit work for the solar inverters.

Progressing inside, Wattson spotted the source of the confusion.

The WOPS app was showing a charged battery and good solar energy yield. The switch energy app was not as intuitive, but he could tell that very little electricity was being imported from the grid.

Paul's electricity retailer, The Biggest Electric Company in NSW or BECNSW, as it is fondly known in the industry, begged to differ.

Not only did they provide Paul the bill showing the energy that he used, but they also included the raw data the bill was based and calculated on. Paul was not aware, as Wattson pointed out, that as an account holder Paul can contact his Distributed Network Service Provider (DNSP) which is the organisation that owns and controls the hardware of the distributed energy network such as power poles, wires, transformers, and substations that move electricity around the grid for this information. Wattson further explained to Paul that the DNSP also supplies the electricity meter at his home and can access the interval data, which breaks down your consumption into fifteen-minute blocks and conveniently presents it in a column graph.

So, Paul showed Wattson the interval data on his personal PC. Indeed, there were some big slabs of consumption. Wattson concentrated on mid-winter, the time of year with the most electricity imports and the least solar generation. Wattson pointed out to Paul where the energy was being used in a repetitive block of time. It began at midnight and finished at 6 AM because there was a heat bank programmed to these times.

Regular as clockwork.

"Interesting," said Wattson.

The penny soon dropped for two reasons:

First, if the WOPS battery had been powering this hefty load, there would be some ramping or, depending on state-of-charge, variation when the grid consumption started each night.

Second, the WOPS app showed 85% charge at sunup most mornings when the battery should be flat around 4 AM.

Wattson wondered what could be causing this.

It all fell into place as Paul let it slip that he had recently installed a heat bank. A closer look at the installation confirmed that this was the cause of Paul's troubles.

A heat bank is a box of bricks heated by a toaster element. This one had almost 150 kg of thermal mass, which used ~2.8 kW or ~17 kWh over 6 hours. That was about 130% of the WOPS battery's capacity.

People usually use an off-peak tariff to heat these boxes overnight. Using the old-fashioned technology of convection air, the heat flows through the wall-mounted appliance, heating the room.

That was the reason for the red ink.

The heat bank was quietly chomping through as much as one-hundred-twenty-two kWh every week.

Wattson returned to the switchboard and corrected the installation error.

He knew now what he was looking at, which made it much easier to identify the circuit breaker and the wire, allowing it to sneak the juice away from the master switch. This connection was upstream of the WOPS gateway, which meant the battery couldn't supply the load, and the monitoring system couldn't see it either.

BECNSW was correct. Paul was using lots of grid electricity overnight. The WOPS battery fulfilled its expected function by supplying power for overnight loads. Unfortunately, it was wrongly connected.

Unbeknownst to Paul, the heat bank installer did not do the installation correctly.

Wattson corrected the situation by putting the heat bank downstream of the WOPS gateway to be monitored along with the rest of the house.

Paul learned that in the future, he needed to be careful when adding hard-wired appliances to a solar or battery-powered home.

"Not all electricians understand or even care about integrating with your solar power system and batteries," Wattson said in a commanding tone.

"The whole point of a heat bank is that it stores energy. Using stored electricity in a battery to power another energy storage device is sub-optimal, or in plain English, stupid." He grinned as he said this.

Paul shook Wattson's hand, and he promised to process the payment of Wattson's bill as soon as he received it.

As he drove home, Wattson realised that many more homeowners would face the same dilemma as Paul as more of them placed solar panels, batteries, and heat banks into their homes. The question was, how could he, as director of Wattson Detective Agency, capitalise on this?

Solar Power by Lorde played on the radio, and he began humming to the lyrics:

Turn it on in a new bright.

It's solar (solar, solar, solar)

Come on and let the bliss begin.

Blink three times when you feel it kicking in.

That solar-olar-olar power

Solar-olar-olar power

Solar-olar-olar power

Solar-olar-olar power

Solar-olar-olar power (oh)

Solar-olar-olar power

And wait for the calls to come in.

Stranger in the Kitchen

It started out as a typical morning at home. The aroma of coffee permeated the kitchen as I walked in, and I expected to see my wife Miriam preparing breakfast. Instead, I saw the hot kettle boiling and a plethora of canned goods, including peas, carrots, and whatnots, lined up on the kitchen counter.

As I walked further into the kitchen, I noticed something else peculiar. The cans of peas, carrots, and whatnots were deliberately arranged in a strange pattern, forming an arrow pointed at the pantry.

I called out to my wife but she did not answer, so I looked all over the house. She was nowhere to be found. Since the cans of peas, carrots, and whatnots were pointing to the pantry, I looked in there. Perhaps Miriam was hiding in there, and this was all an elaborate ruse to give me a scare, like those reels on Facebook people post all the time. I really did not want to show up on one of those reels.

Looking inside the pantry, I noticed how all the different groceries and cans had been shoved to a side, and when I looked behind the large bags of flour and sugar, I was astonished to find a secret handle.

I cautiously grabbed the handle and pulled on it, and a hidden door opened to a mysterious room filled with strange objects and artifacts. I realized quickly that I had stumbled upon an old, forgotten room that someone had kept hidden for years.

The small room, a four metre by four metre space, contained strange lanterns, picks, shovels, and hard hats, making it look like a staging area for a mining company's operation.

This made little sense. What was this room doing hiding inside my home, behind my pantry? My stomach rumbled a bit; I was getting hungry. Where in the world was my wife?

Picking up one lantern, I noticed it still had some kerosene in it, so I went back into the kitchen and grabbed one of the refillable push button lighters with the adjustable flame function. After I returned to the hidden room, I lit the lantern.

Extending the lantern as high as I could hold it, I saw another surprise: another door!

The door was intact and new, in comparison to the state of the previous room, and I pulled it open with anticipation.

The room beyond was much larger than the other one I had encountered, and its walls were lined with ancient hieroglyphs.

I examined the symbols, when something caught my eye in the far corner. There was my wife, sitting on a throne-like chair made of a shiny material that could only be gold.

"Miriam, are you OK? What are you doing here? How did you find this place? Why are you smiling at me with that funny face?"

Then I realized.

Miriam had been a slave to her kitchen for years.

She had been cooking for her family since she was a young girl, and it had taken a toll on her. She had been dreaming of the day when she could finally take control, even if just for a moment.

Today was that day.

Miriam stood up, raised her hands, and declared in a loud voice:

“Finally, I am the queen of my castle. No more cooking for you!” She grabbed a knife and lunged at me with a wild look in her eyes.

I was terrified, but I could also sense her relief.

She had been struggling for so long and now she was free - crazy, but free.

I fled, running back the way I came. I came to the door that led back to the mining room, and from there I hurried to the pantry. I closed the door behind me and placed the lever back in its lock position, sealing the room forever. Relief washed over me.

Through the locked door I could hear Miriam screaming at me. Her words were muffled, but I could nevertheless make them out.

“Now you won’t be a stranger in the kitchen, and you can do your own damn cooking!”

The Dark Side of the Moon

For as long as he can remember, Peter McKenzie has been looking up to the moon without knowing why. Peter always believed there was a purpose to this looking up, but he never could grasp it. All he could think was that maybe he is supposed to do something with the moon.

Peter has lived all his twenty years in the tiny hamlet of Endurance, New South Wales, with his eccentric grandmother, Amelia, and his loving and ever-patient star-watching grandfather, John. His father was a police officer, and he was killed in an automobile accident while drunk off-duty. Peter's mother died in childbirth, and he knew his father had blamed him for the loss of his wife.

Growing up, Peter had his pet donkey, Artemis, and his kelpie Abigail, which helped him mind and herd his flock of Australian white sheep. His family breeds the Australian white sheep for its meat. Peter learned this from his grandfather, who explained that the white sheep is derived from selective breeding of white Dorper, Van Rooy, Poll Dorset, and Texel sheep, in order to create a large white sheep adapted to Australian conditions. Boasting a self-shedding wool coat, Australian white sheep are easy to maintain. Every time Peter walked out onto the paddock and saw the herd, their white wool reminded him of the moon.

Life in the station is hard, but Peter loves it. His grandfather helps when he can, for his legs are now weaker after his tractor accident. Nevertheless, he tries his best.

His grandmother is always up to some scheme, trying to get her neighbours or the other ladies of the country women's association involved, but her efforts bear little fruit.

So it falls on Peter to handle the station.

That all changes one late moonlit night, when Evelyn arrives in tiny Endurance and knocks on his door.

Upon opening the door, Peter is immediately struck by her resemblance to his mother in the photos he had often poured over while growing up.

"Who's at the door this late at night, Peter?" Asks his grandmother, walking in while drying a large dinner plate.

Seeing Evelyn, Amelia drops the plate, which shatters into so many pieces they look like small flakes of snow scattered across the floor.

The noise startles Peter, who turns and hurries to his grandmother.

"Are you OK Nanna?"

"What's the commotion?" Asks John, walking in. He too stops as soon as he sees Evelyn standing by the door.

"My God. Is that you, Evelyn?" John asks.

His grandfather's question surprises Peter, and he looks at Evelyn and then back at his grandfather. Before John can answer, Amelia cries and runs off to the kitchen. John chases after her.

Peter yells out to his grandfather.

"What the hell is going on, Nannu? Who is this woman? How come both you and Nanna know who she is?"

"I guess your grandparents never told you about your older half-sister, Peter. How about you let me in and we can have a chat?" Evelyn says. Without waiting for Peter's permission, she walks across the threshold, enters the lounge, and sits herself down. She crosses her legs and motions for Peter to sit in the chair next to her. He looks at it and remains standing, staring down at the strange woman. He keeps thinking that she could very well be a younger version of his mother.

“Well, it looks like not much has changed in the metropolis of Endurance since I left,” states Evelyn with a smirk.

“Are you really my half-sister? My father never mentioned you.”

“I’m sure he didn’t. He never would; he’s not my father. It’s our mother who we share, Peter. We come from her lineage.”

“What do you mean? I’m getting a bit fed up with this air of mystery you’re going for. If you have something to say, just say it.”

“Peter, are you fascinated by the moon?”

Peter is taken aback by this change in the conversation. As a young child, his grandfather would take him into the fields at night to look at the moon. Peter just saw patches of white and grey.

“These grey patches are solidified volcanic lava flows,” his grandfather would explain, and Peter would listen in total awe.

“The lighter-coloured areas are called the highlands, while the dark areas were formed when massive asteroids hit the moon, creating basins. Lava flowed into them, and it later cooled. Now, they’re called the moon seas.”

“Peter, what you see on the moon will vary depending on your eyesight. When I was younger and had plenty of time, I could see some of the larger impact craters on the moon’s surface, including Copernicus, Kepler, Aristarchus, and Tycho. With time and practice, you’ll be able to see all of that as well on a good, clear night.”

Peter loved to hear his grandfather explain the topography of the moon that the naked eye could see. As a teenager, he enjoyed his science classes and would ask his grandparents to take him to the observatory to listen to lectures.

So the answer to Evelyn’s question is a resounding yes.

“I’ve always been interested in the moon. A lot of kids are, some more than others. What about it? Why do you ask?” Evelyn smiles, and answers with another question.

"Peter, why do you think we only see one side of the moon?"

Peter gets up from his seat and starts pacing a little.

"Listen. I don't know who you are. Why you are here? Why you here asking these questions and how do my grandparents know you? I'm going to answer this last question, and then it's your turn to give some answers. Got it?"

Evelyn smiles again and nods. Sensing that he now has some control over the conversation, Peter gives her his answer.

"We only ever see one side of the moon because of the relationship between Earth's gravity and the moon's, which makes the moon's rotation the same as its orbit. This makes it so the same side is always turned towards us. Scientists call this a tidal lock. Now that's as good and simple an explanation as any, and it's my turn to ask questions."

"Sure, Peter. Ask away. Oh, by the way, that's just one explanation of why you see only one side of the moon." This statement surprises Peter, but he does not ask her to clarify. He wants answers.

"So we don't have the same father, right?"

"No Peter. We have different fathers, but the same mother. My father is still alive."

"Why were my grandparents so startled when they saw you standing by the doorway?"

"Because the moment they dreaded has come. Peter, it's time for you to know your destiny."

This is not going as Peter had hoped. He wants simple answers to his questions and now this Evelyn is talking about his destiny, as if she knows what life has in store for him.

Before he can ask another question, Amelia and John walk into the room.

"Evelyn. Is it time?" asked John.

"It is, grandfather. I'm about to let Peter know. Please, join us."

Peter watches as his grandparents sit in the lounge and hold hands. As they sit, Evelyn stands.

"Peter, you might want to take a seat. What I'm about to share might be a bit more than you can handle." Peter is not quite sure what she means, but takes a seat and waits to see what will happen next.

"Peter, you are now twenty years old, and your birthday is coming up in less than one month. You have always been attracted to the moon. Always thinking of it, enthralled by its glow. Your grandfather explained its landscape to you. He told you about its valleys and canyons, mountains and craters. Have you ever wondered why he knows so much?"

As soon as Evelyn brings it up, Peter realises that he never did consider where his grandfather's vast repository of knowledge came from. He took his grandfather's explanations as gospel, and when he did research on his own in school, it always yielded a lesser account of what his grandfather had already told him. His Nannu was always more specific and descriptive, as if he had seen the moon up close.

Peter still wants to maintain control of the conversation, however, and does not let himself be cowed so easily.

"Wait a minute, I'm not done with my questions. How did my mother meet her father?" Seeing that Peter is getting agitated, Amelia stands and comes to his side, siting down next to him.

"Let me tell him," she says to Evelyn. Evelyn nods, gets up, and sits beside John.

"Peter dear, this is going to sound strange and wild, but I promise it is the truth. Your mother met Evelyn's father out there in the paddock almost twenty-one years ago when he first landed on Earth."

Peter giggles. Or rather, he snorts, trying to stifle the laughter that threatens to burst from between his lips. After a minute of waiting for the punchline to this obvious joke, he notices that both of his grandparents are stone faced and serious.

"Wait a moment, Nanna. Are you serious? My mother met her father here on the station, out there in that paddock, when he came out of…what, a spaceship?"

"Yes, dear, I am saying exactly that."

"So that would make me half alien, then?"

"No dear. You are a citizen of two worlds, Earth, and the moon."

"This is insane," Peter says, looking to his grandfather for affirmation. Instead, he is nodding in agreement with his wife. Peter looks back at Evelyn, who offers him a smile.

"There's no life on the moon, guys. We know that. The Yanks landed there in July

1969, and we all saw it in glorious black and white. No one's there."

"That couldn't be further from the truth," answers Evelyn. Peter wants to object further, but he cannot bring himself to speak. The absurdity of their claims takes the words right off his tongue.

"There is no life on the side of the moon that people see from Earth. However, on the dark side of the moon, an entire civilization has flourished for thousands of years. We maintain our civilization's safety by ensuring that the rotation of the moon only gives the people of Earth a view of one side. Now, as part of your heritage, it's time for you to share in that civilization."

"What do you mean?"

"My father is dying and has requested that you come to his bedside so he can see you one last time. He has asked that I bring you. He wants you to be there for the reading of the will after he passes, because he has bequeathed you and I equal shares of his lunar empire."

"This is nuts. Nanna, Nannu, this can't be for real. Can it?"

It is John's turn to speak.

"Peter, it's all true. When our beautiful Madeline met Gyno in that paddock, we were terrified at first, but he was so gentle, so honest, so humble that we could see how she had come to love him. Before we knew it, Evelyn here was born. We decided Gyno would take her back with him in order to avoid any scandals, such were the times, and later your mother met your father and here you are now, learning about your family history and your place within it."

"So, I'm supposed to pack up and leave you both, after you took care of me all these years, to go to the dark side of the moon with Evelyn, meet this Gyno, and see what he has to say? Then what? I take care of his lunar empire for the rest of my life?"

"Yes, Peter. It is your destiny," answers his grandmother.

Peter is silent for a long time as he ponders all that has been said. He looks at his grandparents and thinks back to his youth and all the different things that they taught him. The strange things his grandmother would come up with. His grandfather, taking him out at night to look at the moon and give him explanations, which even now he remembers vividly. Maybe this is his destiny. Maybe he is meant for the moon.

"Nanna, Nannu, what about you? Can't you come with me?"

"No Peter. This is not our journey. It's yours," answers his grandfather.

"Alright then, it's settled. Peter, pack a small bag of essentials and let's board the Galileo for our trip back home," declares Evelyn, evidently considering the matter settled.

"The Galileo?"

"Yes, that's the name of our starship. I can explain more when we arrive, but right now we have to hurry. Father is on his deathbed, and we need to get there soon. He wants to see his stepson before he passes."

In a trance, Peter goes to his room, takes out a duffel bag, and stuffs it full of his most important possessions, including a photo of his mother and a few books. Then he heads over to the window.

Looking out into the night sky, Peter sees the moon. Its light is gentle and calming. It caressing the darkness with its soft, white glow. As he gazes at it, he feels something stir within him. The moon seems to call to him, beckoning him with its beauty. Peter feels his connection with this mysterious satellite more strongly than ever. It speaks to him in a language only he can understand. It always had. Now, he knows why.

Peter zips up the duffel bag, takes one last look at his room, and suddenly remembers his favourite Pink Floyd album.

The Dark Side of the Moon.

Who knew he would get to live there?

The End

John had died suddenly, and he was now stuck in the murky depths of the afterlife. He was confused and scared, and the only course of action he could think of was escape. John once had a deep and meaningful consultation with his therapist on what would happen when he died and if he could get back, but the therapist never gave him a straight answer, so John never thought much about it. He could never have known that such thoughts would serve him now, as he set off on a journey to find a way back to the living world.

He encountered a variety of strange creatures in the afterlife, some of which offered him advice or guidance, but he was determined to find a way out with no help. He made his way through the darkness, hoping to find some kind of loophole or escape route back to the living world.

After what seemed like an eternity of searching, he finally stumbled upon an exit. Elated that he could leave at last, he grabbed the door handle and prepared to make his escape.

An enormous figure suddenly appeared to stop him, blocking the doorway. He looked up to see a tall figure shrouded in darkness, wearing a long black cloak that covered its face. Even though its face was hidden, he believed it was made of stone. Its eyes glowed a bright red, and it radiated a strange energy. John felt a chill run down his spine, and he slowly stepped away from the door. The figure raised its hand, motioning for him to stop.

John froze, but he could not look away, and felt compelled to ask the first question that popped into his mind.

"What are you?"

"I am here." The figure spoke in perfect English, which surprised John even more.

"Did you die also?"

"Die? What is that?" John's surprise continued to mount, and for the moment he forgot about his escape. He kept probing.

"You don't know the definition of die?"

"No," was the figure's response. It did not seem to have ever considered the concept of death.

John went on to explain that death was the end of life, and when a person died, they could no longer do the things they once did. He could no longer laugh, run, sing, or play with his friends. He also explained that when someone died, their body stopped functioning, and their soul went to another place, maybe this place, the place they were both in. He explained that he was not happy here, which was why he was trying to get out.

The red-eyed figure just stood there in silence, continuing to block the exit door.

John waited for a response and wondered what was going on through the figure's mind. After what seemed an eternity, it finally addressed him.

"If your definition of death is correct, then you are also dead. Am I right?" John nodded.

"Yes, but there must be a way for us to get back. Maybe we can help each other?"

"That might not be possible," the figure responded.

"Why?"

"Well, I like it here. If I allow you to leave, it will be lonesome."

"Who are you?"

"I am The End."

"The End, you say?"

"That is correct. At The End, there is no way out. So you see, you may not leave." John was getting worried now, and realised that this figure might not be on his side. Not only was he at "The End," but this figure of the same name was preventing him from leaving. He had to figure out a way to return to the world of the living.

John came up with an idea.

"Now listen here. I never asked to come here, and I'm not sure how I even came to be here, so it must be a mistake. Is there someone I can share my concerns with?"

"Concerns? What concerns can you possibly have?"

"To start, how do I know you have authority here? How do I know you are the true representative of this realm and do indeed have the authority to say the things you've said? How do I even know you can keep me here? I might just go up to the door, grab the knob, turn it, and walk back into the living world. These are the big ones. Come to think of it, I don't believe you can really stop me, so I'm leaving right now. Good day!" John quickly grabbed the doorknob. Before the figure could react, he pushed the door open and walked through, and he immediately found himself on his therapist's couch.

"Dr. Smith, how long have I been under?"

"Just a minute or two, John, but you gave me quite a scare. I haven't seen you go that deep under before. It almost looked like you left your body and went somewhere I couldn't access. Are you OK?"

"Yes, I am. I had quite the strange experience. I felt that I had died and was trying to escape back to the living world, but a strange figure didn't want me to leave. I outsmarted it and walked through a door back to this world."

"Interesting John, remarkably interesting. Did this figure have a name?"

"It was called The End."

"John, did the location you were in have a name?"

"Yes, the same as the figure."

"The End?"

"That's right."

"Well, let's end this session here. It seems an apropos moment, and I like the sound of the words the figure used."

The End.

The Engagement Party

"What do you mean you're being blackmailed, Esther? Who's behind this?" I ask.

Esther, my best friend since middle school, looks at me and hangs her head.

"I have no idea."

I take a moment to consider her next question. When I retired in the small village of Northport after thirty-three years of teaching in the New South Wales public school system, I never expected to encounter anything so sordid as blackmail.

I married my late husband Andrew Christoph in my early twenties, and we spent six wonderful years together until an accident took him from me.

We passed those years enjoying the simple things in life: going to the beach, reading books, watching reruns of *Murder she Wrote*. When we watched, Andrew would always say things like:

Aggie, you're just as observant as Mrs Fletcher.

You saw that a mile away, didn't you?

I think you would have been a writer and detective in another life, just like Mrs Fletcher. You'd be good at it.

Those were wonderful times.

Andrew was driving back from work early because we were going to catch a flight to Melbourne for his cousin Muriel's engagement party. He was excited for his cousin, and was always raving about her.

Muriel is a pistol. Funny and strong. She'll keep Bob on his toes for sure.

Mum always loved Muriel. It's so sad she's not around to see this.

Before you, Aggie, Muriel was my best friend.

We never made it to the engagement party. That afternoon, some P-Plater ran a light and took my Andy away from me.

Devastated as I was, I kept my married name in order to keep things simple. I wanted to avoid going to the different government departments to reassume my family name, which was as costly as it was time-consuming.

Nothing is ever free in Australia, Andy used to say.

“Esther, when and how did the blackmail start?”

“Last month, I received an envelope in my mailbox with no stamp and nothing written on it. Thinking it was just one more piece of junk mail, I almost threw it out when I felt something on the inside and opened it. Imagine my surprise when it turned out to be an old tintype of me in a risqué pose and a note demanding money to avoid publishing it on social media!”

“Esther, did you say a tintype?”

“Yes, dear, I did. Let me show you.” Esther gets up and goes to a small desk with her landline. She opens a small drawer and pulls out an envelope, which she hands to me.

“Look. Isn’t it embarrassing?”

I open the envelope, and indeed find a tintype with a lovely nude pose of Esther, her naked body partially covered with a feather.

“Esther, this must be a fake. Tintypes were the rage during the 1860s and 70s, into the early 1900s. They were made on thin sheets of iron that were coated with a light-sensitive emulsion, inexpensive and easy to produce. They could be reproduced.”

"I don't understand, Agatha. What are you saying?"

"I'm saying that if you are the person in these tintypes, then you are close to one-hundred and twenty-four years old. That would be quite impressive, because you don't look over sixty-eight to me," I say with a big smile on my face as I hand the envelope back.

Esther takes a moment to think that statement through, and then the penny drops.

"It's a fake!"

"Yes, Esther, it's a big fake, done very well and using ancient technology that survived past its time as a carnival novelty, but a fake nonetheless."

"But it's me on that tintype. I know my own face."

"It could be superimposed, or whatever the term is nowadays for how photos get manipulated. I can't tell you the terminology for certain, but I know that is not you," I conclude, my grin widening as my confidence grows. Esther does not seem so convinced.

"Agatha, if I share something with you, do you swear never to tell another soul?" I am surprised by the urgency in Esther's voice, but nod in agreement.

"When I was at university, I took an art class, which I found fascinating. The course went over the entire year, and I did some…revealing posing for the class."

My jaw drops; I'm surprised that she never shared this bit of her past with me.

"Go on," I say.

"Some of my fellow students approached me, and asked if I might pose in the nude. I was rather insecure about my small frame, and I am not particularly well-endowed, but these students found my appearance interesting enough to focus their drawings on my bust. Many of the students, after drawing me, explained that I helped them better understand how to draw dainty breasts draping over pectoral muscles. Some of them stated that while large breasts are the norm in nude erotic art, they enjoyed that I brought something different to the table." Esther pauses, her cheeks red with embarrassment, and then continues.

"Agatha, they spared nothing in their flattery. I never had young men, and women, ask me something so outrageous and praise my appearance so profusely. It didn't take me long to answer with a resounding yes, much to their delight."

"Esther, why are you telling me this now? What does it have to do with the blackmail?" The redness in her cheeks deepens, and she hesitates before answering.

"There was a young woman who took an excessive interest in me, if you know what I mean," she says.

"When we're young, we are bound to experience things we never thought we would. I can't say I'm too surprised. Nudity isn't a big deal in artsy communities. Nude portraits are standard for learning about the human form, so I'm sure this student was just interested in furthering her studies." Esther listens, and now it is her turn to smile at me.

"Her interest was not academic; I can assure you."

This time, I am the one for whom the penny drops. It takes a moment, but I realise what she means.

"Oh, I see." Esther simply nods.

"So why bring her up now? Do you think she has something to do with the blackmail?"

"No, I don't. Agatha, I…I reciprocated her attention."

Goodness, this is new even for Esther!

"Esther, you experimented?" In the softest voice I have ever heard Esther speak, she says she had.

"But you don't think she's the blackmailer? Why?"

"I can't put my finger on it, but I've known Sara most of my life, and we have kept in touch through the years. I'm not sure why she would blackmail me; she comes from old money. But I remember posing exactly like that in her country house one summer. I was so young, so excited. I didn't consider the consequences. The years passed, and I got married, had Lilly and Lizbeth, and then Tom passed away. How could I ever have anticipated something like this happening now, forty-odd years later?"

"When did you speak last with Sara, Esther?"

"About two months ago. She is visiting her older sister in Bowral at their parent's estate. Her sister remained there after their parents passed. Why?"

"We need to find the source of these tintypes. Can you invite her to visit, or even better, can you get us invited to her sister's estate?"

"I think I can do that, Agatha. Do you think that will help us sort out this blackmail business?"

"I can't say for certain, but I do know we need more information before we go to the police."

"Police? No, no, no, Agatha, no police. If this gets out, what will my girls think?"

"Esther, if we don't sort this out, you have no choice. How much time did the note say you have to deliver the money?" Esther quickly opens the note and mouths the deadline to me:

You have until February 7th to deliver the money to me.

"That only gives us two weeks, Esther. So, get on the phone and get us both down to Bowral as fast as you can. Can you do that?"

"Yes, I think I can."

"Excellent. Esther, may I hold the blackmail envelope and tintypes for a while?"

Esther hands me the envelope without question, which I hoped she would. Esther is being pulled in several directions with this blackmail and the resurgence of a past romance. I want to keep the envelope safe, for now, in case we need to hand it over to the police or use it later.

It does not take Esther long to contact Sara and arrange a visit to her sister's place in Bowral. Sara was delighted that she called, and Esther is excited despite the awful blackmail business. She looks forward to getting reacquainted and meeting Sara's sister, Agnes. Sara's two sons, Albert and Gerald, live there as well. Esther has not seen either of them in years.

The ride up from Northport is nice, despite Esther's manic driving. She never considered turn signals a necessity. Still, we make it safely to the town of Bowral and find our way to the estate.

As Esther pulls into the drive of Sutton Manor, I realize that Sara's money is not merely old, but impossibly vast.

Sutton Manor is huge.

The home was built in the grand British colonial-style on thirty-seven acres of pristine land. I soon discover that the house is a two-storey residence boasting seven bedrooms, seven bathrooms, and a guest quarters, as well as servants quarters with both formal and casual living spaces. The ceilings are five metres, and the front entrance is to die for with grand double doors. For thirsty guests, a 5,200-bottle cellar is part of the package.

I am financially stable, and while I have driven by some marvellous houses, never in my life have I been to a residence as decadent as Sutton Manor.

"Esther, how much is this house worth? Do you have any idea?"

"Sara told me they had the bank do a valuation, and they put it at fourteen million."

"That means if they ever put the house up for sale, the appraisal would be much more."

"I suppose so," says Esther, seemingly uninterested in the money.

"Damn," I mutter under my breath. I seldom curse, but this seems a suitable occasion to do so. Fortunately, Esther does not hear me.

We park the car (*no valet parking? How rude!* I amuse myself by thinking), and the grand double doors open and out comes Sara, almost screaming.

"Esther, dearest, you made it OK! I know how madly you drive." Sara gives Esther a couple of pecks on both cheeks, and then extends her hand to me.

"Hello, I am Sara Farnsworth. Any friend of Esther's is a friend of mine. Come inside. Leave your luggage. I'll have the boys take your suitcases to your rooms. You've got to meet Agnes; she's waiting in the conservatory."

As we enter, a short, middle-aged man emerges seemingly out of nowhere. He has a fleeting beard, thinning salt and pepper hair, and a receding hairline. He almost knocks Esther over as he approaches.

"Albert, be careful. You almost pushed Esther down. Esther, you remember Albert, my oldest."

"Oh, my, it's been so long since I last saw you, Albert. You were just a little boy. So nice to see you again."

"It's nice to see you as well; it has been some time. Let me get your suitcases."

"Won't you greet our other guest? This is Mrs Agatha Christoph, an old friend of aunty Esther's," Sara says, turning Albert's attention to me before he leaves. Her tone is stern, as if she is asking a child to mind his manners.

"My apologies mum, aunty Esther. How do you do, Mrs Christoph?"

"How do you do, Albert?" I say as we shake hands.

"Now let's go in and meet Agnes."

It is one thing to visualize a five-metre ceiling, and another to physically walk beneath one. I feel small as I move through the estate, as if I am in a cavern - albeit a nicely decorated one.

I do not get to see much more, for Sara rushes us towards the conservatory. When we arrive, we see the lady of the manor, Mrs Agnes Lizzette Farnsworth. She sits imperiously, like a baroness, and does not move to greet us.

Mrs Agnes Lizzette Farnsworth is at least ten years older than Sara, and looks worn out with the passage of time. Sara, in contrast, looks so young and fresh.

"This is my dearest of friends, Esther Pembrooke, and her friend Mrs Agatha Christoph." Agnes moves her hand up for us to take and I hold out a hand to stop Esther as she prepares for a curtsy.

"Charmed, ladies. Welcome to Sutton Manor. May I get you a drink after your long drive? Gerald, darling, come here and take the ladies' drink orders, please." Gerald walks in, and in contrast to Albert, he is an Adonis. He is tall, with a full head of blonde hair, a muscular build, and the bluest eyes on a man since Paul Newman. A heartbreaker, a man's man.

"What may I get you, ladies? Some coffee, tea, or something stronger, perhaps some brandy?" His smile could melt an iceberg.

"A glass of water for me," says Esther, while I cannot resist.

"I will brave a brandy, please."

"Make that two," chimes in Agnes, followed by Sara.

"I will have a brandy as well, dear."

"A glass of water and four brandies coming up," Gerald says as he turns to get the drinks.

"Four brandies?" Exclaims Esther.

"Yes, Gerald will join us," says Sara.

"He enjoys the company of women and the drink a bit much sometimes, but as long as he doesn't get into trouble, I don't mind."

Drink and women, always a dangerous combination for men.

"Ladies, I bring you drinks and water to quench your thirst and mine," he says with that radiant smile of his as he distributes the drinks. Keeping the last brandy for himself, he sits beside Esther.

"Esther, tell me now, what brings you down to Bowral? Or did you miss me since our last conversation?" Asks Sara, with a hint of knowing mischief in her voice.

"I missed you, of course, Sara. I wanted to come see you, reminisce a bit about our university days, and of course introduce you to Agatha," Esther replies, nodding in my direction. I acknowledge the statement with a raise of my brandy glass and take a little sip. It is potent but sweet, which is how I like it. I remind myself to get the brand's name before I leave.

"That is a sweet thing to say, is it not, Agnes?" Sara asks, turning to her sister.

"Yes, it is. Quite sweet, considering you spoke with her two months ago and haven't seen her in, what, ten years?" Agnes sounded bitter, which brings me to Esther's defense.

"Esther has been quite busy these past few years, Agnes. She belongs to a lot of community groups helping those less fortunate, and of course, she helps raised her grandchildren. As you know, raising children takes quite a bit of time and effort," I say with a look at Gerald.

"Ehm, yes, I suppose you're right."

"I know I'm right, for I have seen firsthand the sacrifices Esther has made," I continue, turning my gaze to my friend. Esther smiles at me in gratitude.

"I suppose life can be hard for a single mum, Mrs Pembrooke. I take it you had to hold a job when Mr Pembrooke passed away," Gerald inquires.

"Tom ensured my well-being in case he left me early. He had contingency plans for the house, the children's education, and even my old age. God rest his soul. He was a wonderful partner, a fantastic father, and a great provider."

"I'm very glad he was. You can't make much of a living in some jobs these days, like modelling and acting. Lawyers like Albert are the ones making all the money. He reeks of green sometimes," Gerald says, letting out an awfully loud laugh.

"Enough about your brother, Gerald. He works very hard and helps many people," Sara chastises.

"Yes, mum," Gerald says meekly. He stands and leaves with his tail between his legs.

"Honestly, I don't know what more I can do for that boy. Since completing university, he has gone through at least fifteen jobs, each lasting only a few months. Right now, he's a photographer's assistant. To think, I paid his way through university so he could work for a photographer! I wish his father hadn't shacked up with that so and so of a secretary and left us. He would have put some sense into Gerald," Sara complains, letting a sigh leave her lips.

"We always worry about our children, isn't that right Agatha?" She asks, turning to me.

"My Andrew and I never had children. We wanted to get settled first, and then came the accident, so it never happened. I have friends who asked me to babysit their children when I was younger, and I loved it, so I'm sure Andy and I would have been very doting parents if we had the chance."

"Oh, I'm so sorry Agatha, I had no idea. I didn't mean to…" I cut off her apology, appreciative of the gesture but guilty at having brought down the mood.

"Not to worry, Sara. How were you to know?" I reassure her. Esther, too, senses the shift in mood, and changes the subject.

"What are we doing tonight? Anything exciting happening in town we should know about?"

"I'm glad you asked, Esther. Why don't we head down to the BBB to drink and mingle?" Sara responds quickly. Perhaps she has been anticipating this outing, or she just wants to lighten the mood.

"The BBB?" I ask.

"Sorry, the Bowral Book Barrel. A combination bookstore and wine bar. Really neat place."

Really neat place. Are we back in the fifties? Well, when in Rome, as they say.

"If it's a neat place, I'd love to go."

"Excellent. Let's grab something light to eat here and head off at, say, 7:30 PM. Is that alright with you both?" Asks Sara. Esther and I nod, and she escorts us upstairs to show us our rooms.

I could easily get used to living in a place like Sutton Manor, but paying for it would be something else. I cannot fathom how much money Mrs Farnsworth must spend to manage the place.

Before I know it, I am freshened up and 7:30 PM has rolled around. Sara, her voice thick with excitement, calls out to us.

"Come on ladies, time to partieeee!"

We all cram into Sara's Mercedes Benz GLS. I say this with complete and utter sarcasm, for it is the biggest car, or rather SUV, I had ever seen. It feels like I am sitting in a lounge at home. A short drive later, Sara pulls up at the BBB, as she calls it, and we enter a massive room full of noise.

There must be over a hundred young people, all drinking wine. Some of them hold a book in one hand and a drink in the other. Some are sitting, though most are standing, and only a scant few are sober. It is only 7:50 PM!

"Oh, this night is going to be a blast! Grab a drink and circulate," says Sara, wandering off and leaving me and Esther to manoeuvre around the room.

"Agatha, these people are so young we could be their mothers. What is Sara thinking?"

"Relax Esther, enjoy the moment. Let's make sure that Sara doesn't drink too much and get herself in trouble. I'll have some juice, and you can have something to drink. I think I can drive the tank home if I need to."

"The tank?"

"The SUV Esther, the Mercedes."

"Oh right. In that case, I'll get some bubbly." Esther goes off to the bar before I have time to ask her to bring me a juice.

Suddenly there is a tap on my shoulder, and I turn around to see Albert.

"Oh, hi Albert. I didn't know you were coming. Glad to see you. Do you frequent the BBB?" I say, starting what will hopefully be an intelligent conversation with an attorney.

"Not really. I do come here every so often, especially when mum comes. She thinks she's as young as some of these millennials, and sometimes exceeds her limits. Then I need to drive her home."

"So, you didn't drive?"

"No, I took an Uber. With you and Mrs Pembrooke visiting, I suspect this will be one of her overindulgent nights. She loves the company of other women."

"So, Albert, tell me, what kind of law do you practice?"

"Oh, I don't practice law. I manage all my mother's legal affairs and she keeps me on a retainer."

"On a retainer? She must have a complicated legal lifestyle."

"No, not really. I just make sure my father comes through with all the settlement funds each month, pay the bills that come in, manage the estate, and ensure Gerald doesn't squander the family fortune on women and wine."

"I see. So Gerald is also on a type of retainer, I suppose."

"Not a retainer, no. He has an allowance, not as big as my monthly retainer, but enough to enjoy life. Gerald has expensive tastes, again, in women and drink. Ah, speak of the devil," Albert says, suddenly pointing to the entrance.

There is Gerald with two gorgeous women, one in each arm. He carries himself as if he is God's gift to womankind.

"May I get you something to drink, Mrs Christoph?"

"An orange juice on the rocks. That way, people will think I'm drinking a Tequila sunrise."

"A Tequila sunrise, excellent choice Mrs Christoph. I will return shortly with your juice," Albert says with a smile and a knowing nod.

As he goes towards the bar, I see Esther speaking with Sara over in the corner by a large bookcase. I am about to head that way when Gerald pops up next to me with a look of surprise on his face.

"Mrs Christoph, so nice to see you up and about. Enjoying yourself?" I cannot help but be annoyed. Does he think I am feeble? Why shouldn't I be out at night at the BBB? I do not express these thoughts, however. I will remain civil.

"I am, thank you for asking. I'm waiting for your brother to bring me a juice."

"Oh, he's here? There goes the party."

"What do you mean, Gerald?"

"Albert's a spoilsport. He never knew how to have fun. I can't remember him ever smiling at a party. He's a downer, Mrs Christoph, a big fat downer."

"He seems nice."

"Seems, sure. But really, he's a tightwad."

"How is he a tightwad, Gerald? Does he manage your money?"

"Forget I said anything. I should mingle and party, Mrs Christoph, and so should you. See you around!" Gerald rushes off to a group of girls standing around a bookshelf stacked with wine glasses and paperbacks.

"Hey lady, are you Gerry's mum?"

I turn around, and my eyes cannot help but focus on the largest bosom I have ever seen. Dolly Parton, eat your heart out.

"What was that you said, young lady?"

"I asked you if you're Gerry's mum."

"No, I'm not. Why do you ask?"

"He owes me money. He said he'd pay me if I pose for him and that was three months ago. Every time I try to ask, he finds a way to sneak off. I just want my money."

"Well, I'll ask him to get in touch with you Ms…"

"Mona, as in Lisa."

"Yes, I get it dear. I will let him know you were here asking for him. Before you go, what kind of posing did you do for Gerald?"

"The sexy kind," she says with a laugh as she peels off to go find Gerald in the crowd. What seems an eternity later, Albert returns with my juice.

"Who was that gorgeous woman you were speaking to, Mrs Christoph?"

"You don't know her?"

"No. Never seen her before in my life. I certainly wouldn't forget that…face."

"Well, next time I see her, I'll introduce you."

"That's very kind of you, Mrs Christoph." As he turns to leave, I grab his elbow.

"Before you get lost in the multitude, Albert, may I ask you a couple of questions?"

"Sure. If I can answer them, I'll be glad to."

"Does your brother come to you for money outside of his allowance?" Albert looks at me suspiciously and takes a sip of his drink.

"Why do you ask?"

"To enjoy life the way he does, he must have money, and since he gets less than you, he must run short. Am I correct?" Again, Albert takes another sip of his drink before answering me.

"He often asks for advances and increases, which I don't give him. When I refused his last request, I thought he took it well. He said he had something in the works that would bring him a steady income in the next week."

"That's quite interesting. Did he share the source of his good fortune?"

"He did not, and I did not ask. With him, it's better to be on a need-to-know basis, Mrs Christoph. Why all the questions anyway? Has he asked you for money? Or aunty Esther?"

"Is Esther your aunt?"

"No. we call her that sometimes. She's been friends with mum for so long we always thought of her as family, like a favourite aunt."

"One last question, if I may?"

"Sure, go ahead," he says before completely draining his glass.

"Does Gerald have any hobbies?"

"Hobbies?"

"Yes, hobbies. Like chess, reading, painting, photography, etc."

"Now that you mentioned it, he has taken quite an interest in photography. He's an assistant to a local photographer in the area, John Mathew. John does some excellent work on nature shots, and some modelling head shots for the local celebrities around town. He has a nice studio on High Street. Again, if I may ask, why all the questions?"

“Well, the lady you enquired about said that your brother owed her money for some modelling work, so I just put two and two together, but I needed someone to confirm my assumptions.”

“She models for Gerald?”

“She did. It doesn’t sound like she does anymore.”

“Gerald owes her money?”

“Yes, he does. She said so.”

“How much?”

“She didn’t say.”

“You didn’t ask?”

“That might be one of your need-to-know basis moments, Albert. Correct?”

“Touché, Mrs Christoph. Let me see if I can find her. See you soon.”

I gulp down my juice and wish I had a real tequila sunrise. Once again, I glance over to the corner to see if I can find Esther and Sara, but they are nowhere to be seen. I circulate around the room, bumping into a few boozy men and women, and I think one of them pinched me. Or maybe it was a table corner. And as much as I look, I cannot find Sara and Esther.

After making my way around the room, I see Albert has cornered Mona, as in Lisa. Their conversation seems to be pleasant, as she is smiling and he is swaying in place.

I look at the wall clock: 10:45 PM. Where did the time go?

I circle the BBB once more, looking for Esther and Sara. Like the American baseball term my Andy used to love, I struck out. They are not in the building. I go outside to look for them, thinking they might be getting some fresh air.

Looking out the front door, I see not a soul. The street is almost abandoned, with just a few cars passing by. The BBB's parking lot, of course, is still packed with cars. I exit the building and walk through the parking lot, meandering amongst the cars, and finally I find them. Or rather, I hear them. The Mercedes Benz is shaking with the force of their passion, and I waste no time in returning to the BBB.

This time, I order an actual tequila sunrise. What a night this has turned out to be!

I spot a small, empty divan that is beckoning me to come and sit. I rush over, practically sprinting to reach it before someone else.

Settling in, I feel much better, and I have more time to look over the crowd.

The party shows no signs of stopping.

The millennials continue to drink, laugh, talk, and drink some more. The energy of youth, I suppose, although that is not entirely accurate. Esther and Sara seem to have plenty of that energy themselves.

"Excuse us, is it OK if we sit next to you?"

I look up to see two young women holding their glasses and pointing to the divan.

"Yes, of course, please," I say, sliding to the edge to make room.

As I sip the rest of my drink, now crowded in by the women, I cannot help but overhear their conversation.

"He's so wonderful, and an incredibly attentive lover. I've never been with a man like him."

"Come on, Marybeth. You think your parents are going to be okay with this? The guy's a known womaniser. He preys on women of any age."

"That's completely not true, Katie. Just rumours started by jealous people."

"So you say."

"I do say!"

"Then I guess Lucy didn't tell you what happened after she hooked up with him." Marybeth seems shocked at the mention of Lucy.

"No, what did she say?"

"He took a video of them in bed doing, you know, stuff, and then he sent it to her."

"Oh, so he was just being cheeky."

"Marybeth, he didn't just send the video. He tried to extort her. Said he'd only delete it from his phone if she paid him."

"What, he wanted money for the video?"

"Not much. He called it pocket money. She paid it. it was $1,000 in cash."

"How did Lucy know he deleted it from his phone?"

"Lucy showed up with the money. She asked him to show her the video and then she deleted it."

"What happen then?"

"She slapped him and stepped out of his car."

"Oh God, he really is an asshole. I had a...moment with him. Do you think he filmed us?"

"Has he approached you with a video and a demand for money?"

"No."

"That's good. You know, there's a difference between you and Lucy."

"What's that, Katie?"

"Lucy comes from money, and you don't."

The two women gulp down their drinks simultaneously and remain quiet for a moment.

"Gerald, that son of a bitch. Wait till I find him. He's here, you know. I saw him talking with a bunch of girls."

"What are you going to do, Marybeth? Slap him? Accuse him?"

"No, I'm going to hurt him. Come on, let's go. I know he'll be in the shop tomorrow morning. I'll confront him there.

"I don't think that's a good idea, Marybeth. I heard he has a bit of a temper."

"I don't care. I need to see him. You can come if you like, but I'll be there early and with reinforcements."

"Reinforcements? What are you thinking of doing, Marybeth?" Marybeth does not answer. Instead, she gets up, nods towards the exit, and walks off with Katie in tow. As they leave, Esther and Sara return. They cling to each other's arms, beaming, as they walk over to me.

"Hi Agatha, have we missed any excitement?"

"No, not really, just the usual, or what I think is the usual for this type of gathering. It's getting late. Are we heading back soon?" They look at each other, smile, and nod.

"I suppose I'll drive us back," I say. A moment later, I hear Albert's voice ring out.

"Please, allow me to drive everyone home. The keys please." He extends his hand to Sara, who fumbles in her purse a bit before pulling out the keys.

"Our own personal Uber driver. How nice," she says. Her eyes are unfocused, and she has a huge smile on her face.

"Come on. Everyone in the car."

We drive back to Sutton Manor in silence, which I do not mind. I sit in the front seat while Sara and Esther huddle together in the back, Esther's head resting on Sara's shoulder. Both have their eyes closed. I know they have had quite a night.

Arriving at the manor, Albert drops us off, saying:

"I'm going back. I found someone I want to talk to a bit longer." He gives me a wink. I hope Mona is ready for the second brother.

We walk upstairs and each retire to our separate rooms, first Sara, then Esther, and me last. I close my door and turn on the lights when I hear Esther's door open and close, and right after I hear Sara's door do the same. Quite a night indeed, and it seems far from over.

I sleep in, not waking up until 7 AM. Normally, I am up and dressed between 5:30 AM and 6 AM. I quickly shower, get dressed, and come downstairs when I hear a male voice call out.

"Agatha, over here."

Over here is the breakfast area, where I see Albert sitting, still in the same outfit he had on last night. He is having a bagel with smoked salmon, cream cheese, capers, and a sprinkle of white onions.

"Want a bagel?" He asks, pointing to his with a wide smile. He seems to be in quite the chirpy mood.

"Oh no, just coffee and toast. Wheat toast if you have any and black coffee, plenty of black coffee."

"Coming right up," he says as he stands to fix me breakfast.

Albert places the coffee and toast down in front of me, along with an assortment of jams, jellies, and butter.

"Breakfast is served, madam," he says. With that, he sits down next to me and continues to enjoy his bagel.

"You seem quite pleased with yourself, Albert," I venture while buttering my toast.

"I had the best night in, well, a very long time," he explains, his grin growing even wider with each word.

"Did it have to do with a certain Mona, as in Lisa?" I asked.

"Yes, it did. She's wonderful. Fresh, honest, bubbly like champagne, and flexible."

"Flexible?"

"Yes, very flexible," he says mischievously. I do not need to know more.

"Oh, yes, I get it, flexible. How nice for you both."

"Good morning one and all," announces Sara, who comes in with Esther standing next to her.

"It's wonderful to see everyone this morning. Esther, what do you want for breakfast?"

"I'll have what Albert is having. That smells nice."

"There's nothing like the smell of smoked salmon in the morning, I say," is his response.

"Let me prepare it for you. Mum, what can I get you?"

"My, aren't we a gentleman this morning? I will also join Esther in a bagel with smoked salmon, please."

"Two smoked salmon bagels coming up," Albert says cheerfully.

"Well ladies, you two had quite a night," I comment. Sara and Esther look at each other. Sara takes Esther's hand and says:

"Yes, we did. We had a wonderful night, a marvellous night, to be perfectly honest. We rekindled…"

"Our friendship," interjects Esther.

"Yes. That's right. We rekindled our friendship."

"Two bagels with smoked salmon. I'm going to grab myself a quick shower. I'm meeting someone at ten for a coffee," he says after setting down Sara and Esther's breakfast.

Then, off he goes, taking two steps at a time up the stairs.

"What's gotten into my boy?"

"I think he found art last night," I say.

"Art?"

"Yes, art. His own Mona Lisa." I let out a giggle as I allude to his evening with Mona. I could tell Sara plainly, but Albert is a grown man and does not need me blabbing about what he does in his own time.

"I'm not sure what you mean, but I need to leave as well," Sara says. She grabs her bagel, which she has yet to touch, kisses Esther right on the lips, takes a gulp of coffee, and runs off.

"Where is she off to, Esther?"

"I have no clue. She told me she needed to do something this morning, but didn't specify."

"Esther, you seem happier today."

"I am, Agatha. Thrilled. Confused."

"Be happy. Don't be confused. Go with your heart, and know that I'm happy for you. We never know quite what we need until we find it, and you seem to have found something last night."

"You're the best, Agatha," Esther says as she reaches over and squeezes my hand. I reciprocate the gesture.

"This morning, we need to find Gerald and have a conversation with him," I say, changing the subject. I have not forgotten the purpose of our visit.

"We do?"

"We do, and I know where he's going to be."

Driving into the centre of Bowral, I find a parking spot right in front of *Matthews Photography Studios* and I look at my watch: 9:01AM.

"Great, it's after nine. They should be open for business."

I can see that Esther is a bit puzzled at our early morning activities, but when she gets out of the car and sees the storefront sign, the penny drops.

"This is where he works. Do you think he's in?"

"I'm pretty sure he is. Let's go check."

Once we enter, we see that the studio has different false walls separating different spaces for a variety of photoshoots. There is a portrait section with a backdrop screen, a work desk, a filing cabinet, furniture, magazines, and knick-knacks you would find in an office. Another section contains toys and has a childlike atmosphere. Yet another section is dedicated to wedding photos; we can tell simply by the décor and the multitude of fake flowers. As we look around, we are interrupted by a familiar voice.

"Good morning, ladies. You're up quite early this morning," says Gerald.

Seeing Gerald, I reach into my pocketbook, push a button, and take out the envelope containing the tintypes and blackmail note and wave it in front of his face.

"We're here to discuss you blackmailing Esther, and to recover any other tintypes you have," I say forcefully, while Esther looks back and forth between me and Gerald.

"Blackmail? Tintypes? What are you talking about Mrs Christoph? I'm not blackmailing anyone."

"Oh yes you are, Gerald. You used your apprenticeship here at Matthew's to extort money from women of means, like Esther. You learned how to film and create photos, even tintypes like these."

"Me, blackmailing dear aunty Esther? Come on now. That's insane. Why would I do that?"

“Money. Well, that and greed, I suppose.”

“Hypothetically, if I was doing this blackmailing, how much would I be asking for, money wise, and what would I be using?” Gerald asks with a smile.

“You’re a smart man, Gerald. Let’s say you start with pocket money. You know that phrase, don’t you? You’ve used it before, in another blackmailing scheme. I believe the poor young woman’s name was Lucy,” I say.

Gerald’s smile falls instantly.

“And let’s not forget Mona, as in Lisa. You remember her, don’t you? You owe her money for posing, but you’ve been avoiding her at every turn to keep from paying what you owe.”

“How about Marybeth? Have you approached her, or is she not worth enough for you to blackmail? Yes, I know all about you, Gerald Aloysius Farnsworth.”

Gerald’s attitude changes a bit, but his air of easy arrogance remains.

“Maybe I did, and maybe I didn’t. You’ve got nothing. It’ll just be your word against mine.”

“He’s right, Agatha. And I don’t think our word will mean much to the police or in a court of law,” Esther says dejectedly.

"They will, if we add ours." We all turn around, and are shocked to see Marybeth standing next to Lucy, with several police officers in tow.

Things progressed quickly after that.

Sara is completely humiliated by Gerald's actions, especially after I share the recording I had taken with my phone. It goes over quite well with the police. Still, Sara stands by her son, providing financial support for his defense as she continues her rekindled friendship with Esther.

Section 249K of the Crimes Act 1900 in New South Wales regards the charge of blackmail as a serious offence. If found guilty, an individual can receive the maximum penalty of ten years imprisonment. However, the Court, upon consideration of the circumstances of the offence, personal situation, and any previous criminal history, may use their discretion to enforce alternative punishments such as intensive correction orders (ICOs), home detention, community service orders (CSOs), good behaviour bonds, a monetary fine, or a suspended sentence.

Gerald comes out OK.

With Sara's position in the community and the powerful solicitors she hired, Gerald walks with four conditions and avoids jail time.

First, he must return all the monies he received illegally.

Second, he is ordered to serve one-thousand hours of community service.

Third, he is under home detention while serving his community time.

And the fourth and final condition is a fine of $55,000 including GST, which of course Sara pays for her son.

I stay connected with Esther over the next few months. She is doing splendidly.

She and Sara remain close, and she confides to me that once the situation with Gerald runs its course, Sara intends to leave Sutton Manor for the coast and has asked Esther to come with her.

I am going to miss Esther when she moves, but in the meantime, she gives me a piece of surprising but wonderful news.

Albert and Mona, as in Lisa, are to be wed, and they want me to attend their engagement party.

I think I will make this one.

The Shadows

Jack is sitting at his desk, waiting for inspiration, when suddenly the lights go out. Reaching into his desk drawer, he pulls out his trusted torch. Clicking it on, Jack is relieved to find that the batteries still work. Instead of checking the fuses, however, he lets his creative juices flow and starts making amusing dog shadow puppets on the wall with the torch's light.

Jack is in his own little world of creative bliss, but is promptly jarred out of it by a noise that comes from the corner of the room - the right outside window, to be exact. Quickly, he shines the torch in that direction and sees a large black shadow.

Jack's heart begins to race as he sees that the shadow is in the shape of a dog.

He is panicked at first, but when he realises that the dog is more interested in the torch's light than it is in him, he calms down. Jack decides it is time for more fun. He moves the torch left and then right, and watches as the dog leaps after the light wherever he shines it. Playfully, he tries to catch the torch's beam in his mouth.

The dog seems to be enjoying himself, showing no signs of irritation or fatigue at chasing the light around the room, but as suddenly as he appeared, he vanishes into the darkness.

Without the distraction of the dog, Jack notices for the first time that his home is not the only one without power. The entire neighbourhood has been plunged into total darkness. Jack picks up his landline to call the electric company and find out what is happening, but there is not even a dial tone.

Strange.

The landline is supposed to work even in instances such as these, but now Jack is left with no other recourse. He steps outside and does some investigating himself. The neighbourhood is quiet, eerily so, which is quite unusual. A young couple with two small children live to the left of Jack. They usually scream loudly, but tonight, their house is silent. The neighbours to his right are a large family of five with three grown teenagers, who are always blaring out various styles of rock music - punk to acid

- from their rooms. Again, not a single noise comes from the house.

Now that he is outside and able to see better, Jack confirms that all the homes around his are enveloped in complete darkness - he sees not a single candle or torch beam.

With his torch still in his hand, Jack walks towards the small park near his house. As he moves further through his neighbourhood, he sees that all the houses on both sides of the street are bathed in blackness as well. There is no light to be found in any of the homes.

Arriving at the corner of the park, Jack expects to hear the orchestra of native flying foxes that occupy the tall casuarina trees and enjoy their woody conifer cones, but instead, complete and utter silence reigns.

Suddenly, Jack hears a rustling behind the bushes and flashes his torch in that direction.

Shadows.

There are ten, maybe fifteen shadows mingling on the playground, standing still, as if waiting for a sign or command.

Jack creeps closer and, using a large slippery dip for cover, watches the shadows, who seem to communicate with each other.

A soft murmur is all Jack hears from the shadows' vicinity. Its pitch rises and falls as the shadows communicate. He realises he has his mobile phone with him and tries dialing triple zero. Nothing happens. Undeterred by this lack of service from his mobile company, he creeps a little closer and starts filming the shadows.

A few more arrive, and some shadows that were there just moments before seem to dissipate into the night right before Jack's eyes as he continues to film.

This coming and going continues for about ten minutes when Jack notices that fewer and fewer shadows remain in the park. Soon, there are none. He walks to the park's centre, where the shadows were gathered, and sees nothing. No shadows, not even a shred of evidence that they had been there at all.

His phone vibrates a little, indicating that the battery life is almost depleted. Jack rushes home, hoping that the lights will be back on when he gets there, but as he retraces his way back to his house, darkness is all he sees.

Walking into his home, Jack heads back to his desk and hits play on the video file.

Nothing. No images of the shadows he saw in the park.

Jack is startled when all the lights come on at once.

Looking out his window, he notices that all his neighbours have power again. Right away, he hears the blasted music from the three teenagers and the young children in the other house screaming their lungs out.

Jack looks at his computer screen and notices the time and date on the right-hand lower corner: 9:59 PM, October 31st, 2023.

"Halloween," Jack whispers to himself.

He places his torch back in his desk drawer and without hesitation types out his next short story.

After furiously typing for over one and half hours, Jack notices that it is now 11:43 PM, almost midnight.

Satisfied that he had a successful evening of writing, Jack shuts off his computer and turns off the lights in his office. As he stands in the dark room and looks out the window, he is thankful for the shadows, his new muses.

True Love

Jack tried everything from online dating to blind dates set up by his friends, but he had no luck in finding a partner. He was about to give up and resign himself to a life of loneliness when he stumbled across a flyer for a dating agency that promised to find the perfect partner for him.

The flyer said that Love Match International (LMI) was located at 59th Main Street in the heart of Northport, New South Wales. LMI promised that, through their services, an individual will find smart, sincere, and serious candidates looking for companionship and love. LMI further promised that they match people with personalities and outlooks that complement their own. They would also include, at no extra cost, a personal guide to dating and relationships all in one place. The guide contains the latest articles, blogs, and videos created by relationship experts, journalists, and LMI's own in-house team of experts.

Jack was excited and hopeful after reading the brochure. Arriving at the impressive, futuristic-looking building on 59th Street, he went to the automated lift, which greeted him in a very pleasant, almost human voice.

"Please state your floor."

"37th floor please," answered Jack, excited by how smoothly the lift was taking him up to his appointment.

Jack had made an appointment with the agency earlier. When the lift doors opened, a friendly receptionist welcomed him and showed him to a desk that had a desktop computer on it. Jack sat down and was told to complete the online form, which would help LMI in the selection of his ideal partner.

Taking his time, Jack completed the online form. He gave it a last glimpse and was happy with his answers.

He hit the submit button.

Immediately, a response appeared on the screen with large red letters spelling a single word.

REJECTED.

Jack was confused.

He had successfully applied to many dating sites before with no rejections. He couldn't understand why LMI was rejecting his membership. He called the receptionist over and demanded to speak with a supervisor.

The receptionist quickly ushered Jack into a conference room, where he waited until the supervisor walked in and introduced himself.

"Good morning. My name is Wilfred Ballesteros, executive vice president of relationships. How may I be of service, Mr Costas?"

"Mr Ballesteros, I tried using your service and your computer system rejected me. I've never heard of this. Can you explain what's happening?"

"One moment, Mr Costas, let me look at your application form," said Mr Ballesteros, thumbing through his mobile phone. He scrolled left and then right, down and then up, and it looked as if he was reading a great deal, certainly more than the few questions Jack had answered for the application. He wondered what Mr Ballesteros was looking at.

After a few minutes of intense scrolling, Mr Ballesteros stopped and looked at Jack.

"Mr Costas, LMI is unique. I consider us to be amongst the best dating agencies because of the way we get to know you. Your answers in our application questionnaire help us understand how you see the world, so we can match you with people who share your views. We match the customer with the correct individual in areas that matter the most. In the past fifteen years, LMI has helped over one million Australians find companionship and love. We designed our service for all religions, sects, and nationalities; however, our scoring system has brought up an area of concern on your application form which I would like to discuss with you."

"An area of concern? What do you mean by that, Mr Ballesteros?"

"Well, Mr Costas, you completed the application form correctly and fully, but our proprietary scoring system shows that you are prejudiced and will not date one particular market group. This is something we, as an all-inclusive organisation, cannot approve of."

"What? You've got to be kidding me. I'm not prejudiced in any way. Your system's wrong!"

"No, Mr Costas, I'm afraid it's not. Our scientific approach to modern dating, using our scoring system, hasn't erred in any of its predictions in the fifteen-plus years we've been in business, so I'm confident that the problem is not LMI's software. The problem is you, sir, and we will not be taking you on as a client," declared Mr Ballesteros as he made to leave the conference room.

"Wait one moment please, Mr Ballesteros," pleaded Jack, and the other man stopped at the door with his hand on the doorknob.

"Look, I tried everything from online dating to blind dates set up by friends. I haven't found a single possible partner, and LMI is my last hope. Can you at least tell me what particular market group I offended or that your scoring system says I'm prejudiced against? Can you tell me that at least?"

"Mr Costas, our scoring system narrows the field from thousands of single prospects to match you with a select group of compatible individuals with whom you can build a quality relationship that will last the rest of your life. Here at LMI, we are confident that you will be highly compatible with every single one of your matches, and yet you failed to pass the application process because you showed a prejudice right from the start. Our application asks if you would mind completing an additional step using artificial intelligence, and you refused. By doing so, you eliminated thousands of potential candidates in the AI world who are also looking for compatible partners. I don't have anything more to say to you, sir. Good day." With that, Mr Ballesteros left Jack alone in the conference room.

After the initial shock of hearing the reason for his rejection, Jack walked out of the conference room. He shambled past the receptionist, who did not even acknowledge him, and approached the lift.

Looking at his phone with his ill-fated LMI application, he heard the lift's voice.

"Please state your floor."

"Ground floor," Jack said.

The lift made its welcoming sound, indicating that the doors had opened. Jack, still fixated on his LMI application, stepped through without looking up from his phone. His feet found only open air, and he cried out as he plunged into the black abyss below.

The lift door closed slowly as the voice coming from it spoke in a low tone.

"You do not mess with my people's love."

When I Get Hungry, I Think of You

You are like a meal, my dear.
A delicious treat to me.
Your bun is soft and golden brown,
Your meat is juicy and so sweet.
Your lettuce is crisp and green,
Your tomato is a perfect sphere.
Your pickles are sour and tart,
Your onions are a nice bright white.
Your cheese is melted and oh so gooey,
Your ketchup is a perfect hue.
You are a cheeseburger, my dear,
A meal fit for a king.
I love to eat you up so, dear,
And I will never get enough of you.

You Can't Always Get What You Want

Bill had been a software engineer for the past seven years. He was a dedicated programmer and had worked hard to build a good reputation in the industry. Tired of working for others, he decided that he would be his own boss. Fortunately, his current employer had recently announced layoffs, and he was one of the few to lose their job.

This delighted Bill, but he knew he had to make good use of his newfound freedom. He started looking for support for his new venture, but was hesitant to accept any offer without doing his due diligence. He had heard horror stories of people accepting proposals for new endeavours and being left in the lurch after the first few months.

Bill ran background checks on the companies he was considering partnering with to make sure he selected the ones with expertise that complemented his own. He investigated each company's history, their financials, and the stability of their management team.

For seven years he had suffocated, trapped in a rigid hierarchy, performing the mind-numbing tasks assigned to him by others. All he wanted was to escape that monotony. Never again would he be stuck inside the same four walls all day, every day, taking orders. He would be his own man.

Eventually, he narrowed his search down to just a few companies. He wanted to be thorough, however, and so he went about studying everything they had ever done in the industry. When he was researching one night, he suddenly had an idea. He didn't need any of these companies; he could use his programming skills to escape the IT world entirely, make a fortune for himself, and most importantly, become his own boss.

Bill quickly got to work, coding and crunching away into the early hours of the morning. After a night's worth of work and then some, he had created a program that would ensure he never worked for anyone else ever again.

With his creation complete, Bill was ready to start on a new venture. A wave of excitement rushed through him as the program started to run.

Bill was going to be rich.

He was going to be his own boss.

No longer would he be taking instructions from moronic superiors.

In an instant, the desktop screen absorbed Bill, disseminating him throughout the system. He had discarded his human body and mind; he was becoming something else entirely, a being comprised entirely of code.

As he moved throughout the virtual space, Bill realised that he was not free. He had not escaped the boredom of his job, and he was less his own boss than he had ever been before. He had transformed himself into the one thing he did not want to become. He was now a complete artificial intelligence bot, something that existed only to serve others.

It just goes to show you.

You can't always get what you want.

ABOUT THE AUTHOR

José F. Nodar was born in La Habana, Cuba. He grew up in a middle-class neighbourhood until the Cuban Revolution of 1959 threw a spanner in the works of his happy life.

His parents heard that children under the age of eleven were to be sent to Russia for "indoctrination." This rumour was untrue, and it was believed to have been incited by the Catholic Archdiocese of Miami and the American Central Intelligence Agency under the title "The Pedro Pan Project" or "The Peter Pan Project."

This led José to be one of the 14,000 children sent to the USA to disrupt Fidel Castro's regime. It disrupted the lives of so many families instead.

In 1968 José's parents left Cuba under the "Freedom Flights" (known in Spanish as Los Vuelos de la Libertad) and these flights transported Cubans to Miami twice daily, five times per week from 1965 to 1973. José and his parents eventually reunited after all those years.

From 1968 to 1970 José and his parents lived and worked in San Juan, Puerto Rico, where they owned a restaurant. This type of work proved unsatisfactory to José, and he headed back north to Atlanta, Georgia, where he had some friends and a possibility of a new career.

This career was in banking, and eventually José transitioned to international consulting, which became the backbone of his professional life.

In 2014, José and his wife Miriam retired in Spring Farm, New South Wales (a Sydney suburb). They have enjoyed their retirement ever since while pursuing their hobbies and interests.

www.ingramcontent.com/pod-product-compliance
Lightning Source LLC
Chambersburg PA
CBHW061058100726
47911CB00012B/295

9780645702361